Enid Blyton

Well Done,

D0663940

Have you read them all?

Enid Blyton

Well Done,

THE NAUGHTIEST GIRL

WHYTELEAFE

CHAO · ET · PERTINACIA

Illustrated by Kate Hindley

Hodder
Children's
Books

a division of Hachette Children's Books

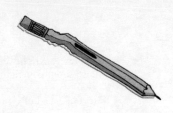

CONTENTS

INTRODUCTION

by Cressida Cowell

bestselling author of the
How to Train Your Dragon series

Like so many, many children before and after me, Enid Blyton's books played a crucial role in turning my nine-year-old self into a passionate reader.

That is because Enid Blyton had an extraordinary knack for writing the kind of books that children actually *want* to read, rather than the kind of books that adults think they *should* read.

Enid Blyton could tap into children's dreams, children's desires, children's wishes, with pin-point accuracy. She knew that every child, however good and well-behaved they might look on the outside, secretly longed to be Elizabeth Allen, the naughtiest kid in the school. I'm afraid I entirely cheered Elizabeth on, as she defied her parents, the headmistresses, her schoolmates, and the very serious School Meetings. If anything, I wanted her to be even naughtier.

But the Naughtiest Girl books were really my favourite of Enid Blyton's school stories because of Whyteleafe, a very different school from Malory Towers or St Clare's. What if there could be a school in which discipline was administered by the children rather than the adults? In which all money was given in at the start of the term and distributed amongst the children along socialist lines? Wouldn't this be the kind of school that children would actually *want* to go to, rather than the kind of school that children *have* to go to?

It was an interesting proposition to a nine-year-old, and it remains an interesting proposition.

I hope you enjoy this story as much as I did when *I* was nine years old.

Cressida Cavell

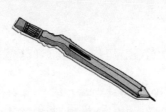

CHAPTER ONE

A NASTY SURPRISE FOR ELIZABETH

'THE LEAVERS' Concert is going to be something very special this year, Elizabeth,' said the music master. 'Very special indeed.'

Mr Lewis was in charge of music at Whyteleafe School and also taught piano, violin and flute. Elizabeth took piano lessons with him but had been excused them for the past few weeks as she had been very busy with the Summer Play. The play had been performed now, so she was free to resume them, but she had almost forgotten her first lesson back. She had had to run all the way to the music room.

'Even more special than last year?' asked the Naughtiest Girl, puffing as she recovered her breath. 'I thought it was such a lovely concert last summer. I really enjoyed myself.'

She undid the straps of her regulation brown leather music case. Then she scrabbled inside to find her sheet music. Which piece had they been working on? She couldn't recall.

'Yes, Elizabeth, I seem to remember you were

1

excellent,' replied Mr Lewis. The elderly music master fingered his beard and looked thoughtful. 'You worked very hard for it.'

Elizabeth felt pleased. She was still basking in the warm afterglow of the first form play. Her interest quickened. How exciting it would be to take centre stage again so soon. The school concert – of course! It was held right at the end of the summer term and parents were invited. Her mother and father would be coming, just as they had last year. Her one tiny regret about the play was that Mummy and Daddy had not been there to see her!

How well she remembered last year's concert, at the end of her very first term at Whyteleafe School. She had started the term as the Naughtiest Girl in the School, hating the idea of boarding-school and doing everything bad she could think of – with the intention of getting herself sent home. But she had ended the term as a proud member of the school, playing two duets on the platform with a brilliant boy called Richard, as well as a little sea piece on her own. She remembered the applause ringing in her ears and the happy looks on her parents' faces . . .

'Why will this year's concert be so special, Mr Lewis?' she asked, as she found a piece of music and sat down at the piano.

'Because we have some very special Leavers this time,' he reminded her. 'Last year, only two or three boys and girls were old enough to leave Whyteleafe but this year there's a whole batch. And what a fine batch they have been. Not just Roger, who's won his scholarship, but Charles and Colin and Lynette and – most important of all – our head boy and head girl. They have been the finest heads we have had at Whyteleafe for a long time.'

'William and Rita!' exclaimed Elizabeth. 'Of course. Oh dear. I just can't imagine Whyteleafe without them. I *do* wish I could make time stand still.'

'But then you would have to stay in the first form for ever, Elizabeth,' chided Mr Lewis. 'And you wouldn't like that, would you?'

She shook her head so hard that her brown curls flew back and forth across her face.

'No, I would NOT!' she exclaimed.

If there was one thing she was looking forward to with all her heart, it was the prospect of moving up in September. It would be brilliant to go up into the second form with Julian and Kathleen and Belinda and all the other boys and girls in the first form who were old enough and clever enough to go up. How grown-up they would feel then! Her friend Julian would have to stop playing so many jokes in class and start behaving

3

like a responsible second former. And it would be lovely to be reunited with her best friend, Joan, who was already in the second form and a monitor. It was all going to be such fun! And if losing William and Rita was the price that had to be paid for time not standing still, then Elizabeth had to be willing to accept it!

'I expect excellent replacements will be found for William and Rita, when the time comes to elect a new head boy and girl,' Mr Lewis was pointing out. 'But, in the meantime, it's been decided to give them a very special send-off. To make the Leavers' Concert one of the best we've ever had. Something for them to remember for ever.'

'How wonderful!' exclaimed Elizabeth. She suddenly felt very excited. What a privilege it would be to play at William and Rita's Leavers' Concert. She thought back to the duets she had taken part in last year. To play with Richard again, some beautiful duets, to be part of William and Rita's last memories of Whyteleafe . . . How thrilling that would be.

'Richard won't be one of the Leavers, will he?' she asked suddenly.

'No! We've got Richard for another year or two yet,' replied Mr Lewis. 'I'm pleased to say. But even Richard won't be the star performer this year. You see, to make the concert extra special, Miss Belle and Miss Best have

4

invited Courtney Wood to come and play, the well-known concert pianist. And he has accepted!' The music master could barely conceal his pleasure. 'Isn't that exciting news, Elizabeth?'

'Oh,' said Elizabeth, dully. 'Won't any of the boys and girls be playing at the concert then?'

'Of course, of course,' replied Mr Lewis, a trifle impatiently. He was glancing at his watch now and turning over the sheet of music that Elizabeth had propped up in front of her. It was time for the lesson to begin. 'But we won't be able to have half as many children as usual. Just one musician from each form. That's all we'll be able to fit into the programme. There won't be any duets this year. The very best child from each form will play, that's all. Richard will represent his, of course . . .'

Elizabeth's hopes immediately rose again. So she still had a chance of being picked, then. And as a solo performer!

She thought about it. In the first form, Harry was keen but not very good – his hands were like a bunch of bananas, Richard often said. Arabella had been learning the piano for a long time but it was well known that she was always in trouble with Mr Lewis for never doing her piano practice. Belinda and Edward were both learning the violin but they had only started last term . . .

'Tut! Tut!' exclaimed Mr Lewis, breaking into her calculations. He was removing the sheet of music from the piano. 'This won't do, Elizabeth. You've put the music on its stand upside-down! And . . . what's this?' He turned the sheet the right way up. 'We finished *Serenade* before half-term. We're on that difficult arrangement of *Greensleeves* now, don't you remember?'

Flustered, Elizabeth groped in her brown music case and found the correct sheet. It was right at the bottom.

'What's it doing buried down there?' scolded Mr Lewis, as he opened it up at the first page and placed it on the stand for her. 'Now, let's see if you've been doing your piano practice.'

It was soon very obvious that she had not.

'Really, Elizabeth,' winced the music master, as she got all tangled up on the opening bars, 'what's happened to you? You were playing that opening beautifully not long ago. And look at the little finger of your right hand, all scrunched up! You'll never reach the high notes like that. Stretch it out wide, S-T-R-E-T-C-H.'

The lesson went badly.

'Elizabeth, you are a very naughty girl,' Mr Lewis said to her afterwards. 'I don't believe you've done any piano practice at all, lately. I don't believe you once went near the piano while you were mixed up in that play of yours. Am I right?'

'Yes, you *are* right,' confessed Elizabeth, looking upset. 'I'm sorry.'

The little girl was too proud to make excuses. She was too proud to explain that going to all the rehearsals for the play, and learning such a big part until she was word perfect in every line, had been a difficult task. There had been other things to worry about, too, which had taken up all her spare time and energy. Though they were all now sorted out, they had loomed large at the time.

In the meantime, not only Elizabeth's piano practice but a lot of her school work, too, had been pushed to one side. She would not have dreamed of explaining this to anyone, for fear of looking feeble.

In any case, Mr Lewis was smiling at her now. He had spoken more in sorrow than in anger.

'Cheer up,' he said. 'I can see you really are sorry and will turn over a new leaf. If you do your practice every day, you will soon make up your lost ground. Practice makes perfect. That's what I'm always saying to Arabella.' He chuckled. 'Yes, that's what I've been telling her for a long, long time.'

Elizabeth mildly wondered what there was to chuckle about, as far as Arabella was concerned. But she was so relieved that Mr Lewis was not being cross any more, she cared not.

'I *will* do my practice every day, I promise!' she said happily, as she packed her music case and prepared to leave. 'When I come for my lesson next week, you will see such a difference!'

'I shall look forward to that, Elizabeth.'

She longed to ask more questions about the Leavers' Concert. In particular, she longed to hear Mr Lewis say that she stood a good chance of being picked to represent the first form. But her good sense told her that this was hardly the right moment. She would ask him next week, when she had had a chance to catch up on her piano practice. He would see how well she was progressing with the difficult new piece. Then, surely, she would be chosen to play it at the concert? It would be such an honour to play it for William and Rita and the other Leavers, in front of the whole school, in front of all the parents! In front of her *own* parents. It was a thrilling thought.

'You're looking cheerful, Elizabeth,' said Julian Holland, as she came into the common room. 'Where've you been?'

The boy with the dark, untidy hair and humorous green eyes pushed his chessboard to one side. He had been working out a few interesting chess moves. But nothing was ever more interesting than talking to the bold, bad Elizabeth. They were great friends.

'Piano lesson,' she replied. 'Here, Julian, have a chocolate biscuit. As a matter of fact, I *am* feeling cheerful.'

'Must have been a good lesson,' grinned Julian.

'Not especially,' replied Elizabeth, airily. She was not going to admit, even to Julian, that she had been unable to cope with her piano practice recently and how disappointed Mr Lewis had been in her. 'It's just that Mr Lewis had some interesting news.'

She told him all about Courtney Wood coming to play at the end of term. And then, even though the common room was empty, she dropped her voice low and confided in Julian her secret hopes.

'I do believe you're getting quite stage-struck, Elizabeth Allen!' teased Julian. 'Not content with being the star of the Summer Play, you've now decided you'd like to appear on the same platform as Courtney Wood!'

There had been a time when the Naughtiest Girl would have flared up at that. But now she just took the joke against herself in good part.

'It's not that, and you know it,' she smiled. 'I'll tell you what it is, it's because of William and Rita. Oh, Julian, I can hardly bear to think that this is their last term at Whyteleafe. I want to practise and practise until I can play my piece really *beautifully*. It's just the right music somehow and says everything I'm feeling and how sad I am at saying goodbye. They've given me so much and helped me to be a better person and . . .'

Julian gazed at his friend in admiration. He could see how sincere she was being. She was struggling to find the right words. He finished the sentence for her.

'. . . so this would be your way of saying thank you? Of giving them something back?'

'Yes, that's it exactly,' said Elizabeth, gratefully.

'Well, I expect you'll be chosen,' said Julian, airily. 'Nobody else in the first form is much good except you, Elizabeth. Least, that's what I've always heard. Blow it, I think I'd like to give William and Rita something myself. I think I'll carve them a little wooden animal each. A Mother Bear and a Father Bear. How about that, Elizabeth?'

'Oh, Julian, that's a brilliant idea.'

'I must start looking out for just the right bits of wood. I say, we *are* going to miss them, aren't we, Elizabeth?'

The two friends fell silent for a few moments.

Elizabeth swallowed hard.

'But it's got to be, hasn't it?' she said at last. 'Mr Lewis reminded me of what would happen if you made time stand still. If William and Rita were just to stay as head boy and head girl for ever and ever and never move on—'

'What?' asked Julian.

'We'd all have to stay in the first form for ever and ever, too,' said Elizabeth, wryly. 'We wouldn't be able to go up to the second form in September!'

'What a nightmare!' said Julian. He laughed. 'Oh, we couldn't stand for that. I don't know about you, Elizabeth, but I can't wait!'

'Me neither!' agreed the Naughtiest Girl.

It was such a happy thought that they both felt cheerful again.

But Elizabeth's happiness was to be very short-lived.

The next morning Miss Ranger, their form teacher, told the class the result of this month's tests. She read out the new positions in class.

Julian had come top, as usual. His cousin, Patrick, had worked hard and come second. Elizabeth, who usually came very high, waited in vain to hear her name read out.

She was in for a nasty surprise.

She had come third from bottom.

Even Arabella, the oldest in the class but usually near the bottom, was two whole places above her. Since half-term she had been working frantically hard and had made her very best effort.

'You will have to do better than this in the end-of-term exams, Elizabeth,' said Miss Ranger. 'Or we may have to keep you in the first form a little longer.'

Elizabeth could hardly take it in. She had been beaten in class by Arabella!

However the sight of Arabella's gloating face made her determined not to show her true feelings.

She spoke airily, almost defiantly. She repeated what Mr Lewis had said to her the previous day, the first words to come into her head.

'I shall soon make up any lost ground, I dare say, Miss Ranger.'

But inwardly Elizabeth was shaking. She had been given a dreadful fright.

CHAPTER TWO

TWO LITTLE PUZZLES

AFTER THAT, Elizabeth decided that she must start revising very hard indeed for the exams. But she didn't want any of her classmates to know what a fright she had been given, not even Julian. She lost no time in finding herself a secret den, somewhere that she could study in peace.

She found the perfect place high up in an oak tree. She was there now.

Above her head came little rustling sounds as two doves moved along a branch. A pair of collared turtle doves, with black half collars round the back of their pale dusty brown necks – they were permanent residents of the old oak, along with all manner of other creatures. The doves were getting quite used to Elizabeth's presence. This was the third day running that she'd been here.

As she began to recite her French verbs, they began to croon, as though to keep her company.

'Je suis . . .

'Tu es . . .'

Coo–cooo, coo

'Il est . . .

'Nous sommes . . .'

Coo–coooo!

Elizabeth's little 'tree house' had been a wonderful find. She was delighted with it.

'I'm quite near the school buildings,' she thought with a smile, 'yet nobody knows I'm here. Nobody can see me or hear me up here. It's my own secret place. Nobody can make fun of me now!'

The way that Arabella had gloated over her plunge down the form order had been almost too much to bear. The two girls disliked each other intensely. Elizabeth hated Arabella's pretty little face and perfect manners, her high opinion of herself and the airs and graces she put on. Arabella despised Elizabeth for her untidiness, her noisy, boisterous ways and the fact that she seemed to get away with things just because people seemed to like her! It puzzled her why they should.

Nor had Elizabeth taken kindly to the teasing from her classmates, even from Julian. The truth was that, unlike Elizabeth, none of them took Miss Ranger's words seriously, about her being kept down in the first form. And Elizabeth had taken such care to hide her true feelings, they had no idea how scared she was feeling.

TWO LITTLE PUZZLES

'What would you like for your next birthday, Naughtiest Girl?' Julian had joked. 'Remind me to buy you a rattle.'

Elizabeth had pretended to laugh. But it was soon after *that* that she noticed the oak tree and decided to explore it.

From the school grounds, only the upper part of the tree was visible, for it stood on the other side of the school wall, somewhere in the outside world. But its heavy boughs brushed the top of the wall in places and some of the branches overhung the grounds.

Elizabeth had peered up into the dense green foliage. How mysterious and cool and inviting it looked up in that oak tree. Its boughs seemed to reach down like great arms, inviting her to come up into the tree's embrace. With a feeling of excitement she realized that, if she climbed to the top of the school wall, it would be extremely easy to crawl along the nearest bough and into the heart of the tree.

As soon as she did so, she knew that she had found the perfect hideaway. Where the boughs met the trunk in the midst of the tree, it was possible to sit, or even lie down, in comfort. Enclosed in a lattice-work of foliage, it was like being in a secret little house – her own tree house. Wonderful!

TWO LITTLE PUZZLES

On her first proper visit, she took her maths book and learnt her eleven times table off by heart.

The next day she took her spelling book and carefully copied out several difficult words until she was sure that she knew how to spell them correctly.

Today, Julian had asked her to help him look for pieces of wood, as he wanted to start on his bear carvings. But Elizabeth had made an excuse and headed straight for her hideout again, this time bringing her French verb book with her.

'Vous êtes . . .'

She cheated and peeked into the book.

'Ils sont!'

She put the book back in her pocket. Then, straddling a bough, her back pressed comfortably into the curve of the tree trunk, she closed her eyes and recited the verb 'to be' all the way through, slowly and carefully. Then again, but faster. By the third time, she was able to rattle through it without stopping.

'There! I know it now!' she thought, with deep satisfaction.

It was so grand to be able to recite things out loud, as many times as she wanted to, with nobody to overhear. It was so peaceful here, with only the natural world for company.

'Hello, robin,' she said, as she opened her eyes.

The bird had hopped along the bough to within a metre. It was full grown but had not yet got its red breast, so Elizabeth knew it must be very young. 'Aren't you the lucky one, then? You don't have to learn your verbs yet, do you?'

The young robin cocked its head on one side and gave her an enquiring look, followed by a friendly chirp.

'I love it here,' thought Elizabeth. 'There's a whole busy life going on in this oak tree and, it's funny, I'm beginning to feel part of it. I'm even beginning to like the big brown moths that live here. And I think the creatures are starting to get used to me.'

She stared up into some higher branches, where a family of squirrels had their drey. On her first visit they had chattered shrilly in great alarm and refused to come out. On the second day they had made their way up and down the tree very secretively, by a back route, hoping not to be seen. But today they had twice scampered down the tree quite close to her, taking no notice of her at all.

She settled further back and rested for a while, gazing up at the chinks of blue sky through the tree's top canopy. From the road below, to her left, came the drone of an occasional car. The mighty oak stood on a grass verge beside a narrow road that led to the village.

And across the school grounds to her right, from the

school buildings, came the sound of a piano being played in one of the practice rooms.

'Oh, that's a nice piece!' thought Elizabeth. 'All ripply and sweet like a journey through the English countryside. That must be Richard playing.'

Piano practice! She had forgotten to do it today!

Elizabeth roused herself and began to edge backwards along the bough, towards the top of the school wall.

As she did so, looking down, she spotted a knobbly little chunk of oak that the tree had shed. It was lying in the grass, close to its roots, not far from the road.

'That's just the sort of wood Julian likes when he's carving things,' she thought. 'It's got an interesting shape. I wonder if I dare get it for him?'

She could see that it was an easy climb down to the ground. The trunk had several low, stubby branches sticking out. They would make perfect footholds and handholds. But, of course, it was strictly against school rules for children to venture outside the grounds on their own.

'Only, I'm not really going anywhere, am I?' Elizabeth told herself. 'Just straight down the tree to pick up the wood for Julian, then straight back up again.'

It took Elizabeth less than a minute to climb down the tree and land on the grass verge on the other side of the school wall. She scooped up the piece of wood, triumphantly. She examined it carefully. Yes, it was a really good piece. Julian should be pleased.

As she turned back towards the tree, she stared in surprise at its trunk.

'How stupid!' she thought.

On its handsome pale brown and mossy green bark, someone had painted an ugly white cross.

At that moment, from beyond the bend in the road, she heard the distant sound of a car approaching. Supposing it were one of her teachers? Help!

Elizabeth shinned back up the oak tree at speed, dived into its leafy branches, bumped along the bough atop the school wall, then down into the grounds of Whyteleafe. Phew! That was risky.

She must not do *that* again.

But as she wandered back towards the school buildings, past the end of the cricket pitch, her thoughts returned to the strange marking on the oak tree's trunk. She wondered why it made her feel uncomfortable. Then she remembered that they had once been told in a history lesson about the time of the Great Plague. How homes were similarly marked with a cross if the disease had struck.

'Could the oak tree have some sort of disease?' she wondered, in dismay. 'Oh, surely not. It looks hale and hearty to *me*.'

She wondered if she could ask one of the teachers about it. In a roundabout way, perhaps. It would be difficult, though, without giving away where she had seen it . . . Oh, surely, somebody had just been fooling about . . . ?

'Elizabeth! Whoops! Look where you're going!'

She had almost crashed into someone! He was a tall boy, carrying a cricket bat.

'Richard! Oh, I'm sorry. I was in such a dream.' She looked at the bat under his arm. 'Going off to play cricket?'

'No! Just coming *back*!' said the senior boy, smiling at her. 'I've had an hour's practice in the nets and that's long enough for me. I must get back to my piano.'

'Oh, I thought I heard you playing a few minutes ago,' said Elizabeth, in surprise. 'A lovely, ripply piece. Perhaps it was Mr Lewis, then?'

'Not him. He's gone to town to buy the piece I shall be playing at the Leavers' Concert. And it doesn't ripple, Elizabeth, I can assure you.'

Elizabeth continued on her way, frowning slightly. Who had been playing that piece so well, then, if it had not been Richard, or Mr Lewis himself?

With something new to puzzle about, she forgot all about the white cross on the oak tree.

CHAPTER THREE

ELIZABETH HEARS THE MUSIC AGAIN

'WHAT AN excellent piece of wood, Elizabeth!' exclaimed Julian, with pleasure. 'Why, it's the very thing.' He rolled it between his palms. 'A solid little lump of oak. I shall cut it in half and make two. Those knobbly bits at each end already look rather like bears' heads, don't they?'

'That's just what I thought, Julian,' said Elizabeth eagerly. 'And one end's fatter than the other – that can be Father Bear.'

'And the other end can be Mother Bear. Excellent! I'm going to enjoy my wood carving! Oak's good to work with, you know.'

After a good wash and tidy-up, Elizabeth had rushed through some piano practice and then come looking for Julian. She had found him in the common room. He was not bothering to revise for exams. He was reading a book about famous medical discoveries.

She had presented him with the piece of wood.

'Wherever did you find it?' he asked now.

'Oh, just lying on the ground,' replied Elizabeth, truthfully.

'You've been gone for ages!' said Julian. 'I wondered where you were.'

'Well, for one thing, I've been doing my piano practice,' smiled Elizabeth.

'Ah, yes.' Julian gave a quick nod.

Some of the other boys and girls were coming into the first form common room.

Julian quickly stuffed the piece of wood into his trouser pocket. He wanted to be quite sure that his bear carvings were successful before letting anyone know about them!

Belinda came and threw herself into a chair.

'If I have to revise another single French verb, I shall die!' she exclaimed.

'Only two weeks to go till the exams now,' said Julian cheerfully.

Jenny came and joined them. She was holding a tin.

'Have some of my birthday cake!' she said.

She cut them each a fat slice. It was a gooey chocolate cream sponge with thick chocolate icing on the top.

'It's delicious, Jenny!' exclaimed Elizabeth, as the cake melted in her mouth.

'I was trying to find you after tea, Elizabeth. Where

do you keep disappearing off to?'

'I can't bear to be indoors at this time of year,' replied Elizabeth, truthfully. 'I've been getting lots of fresh air.'

'I expect she's been helping John over in the vegetable garden,' put in Kathleen. 'That's where she usually disappears to!'

Elizabeth had no need to reply for Belinda at once jumped in with a teasing remark.

'I'm sure I'd be revising for exams if I'd come third from bottom! But there again, I'm not Elizabeth. I'm not the Naughtiest Girl!'

'Blow the silly old exams,' said Elizabeth, keeping up her brave front.

But it was very satisfying in the maths lesson next day. Miss Ranger gave them some mental arithmetic problems. Twice Elizabeth was the first to call out the correct answer.

'Eleven boys have to share out eighty eight sweets equally. What does each of them get—?'

'Eight, Miss Ranger!' cried Elizabeth.

'Tummy ache!' cried Julian.

Everybody laughed.

'That will do, Julian. Well done, Elizabeth. And if twelve rabbits have to share out one hundred and thirty two lettuce leaves equally, what do they get—?'

'Into a fight!' exclaimed Patrick Holland, determined

not to be outdone by his smart cousin, Julian.

The laughter was more subdued this time, as Miss Ranger was beginning to look cross.

'Please, Miss Ranger, eleven lettuce leaves,' said Elizabeth, putting her hand up.

'Yes. Good.'

Belinda sighed to herself. Elizabeth was so lucky. Without appearing to do any work, she was getting back into top form again. It was all right for some!

However it was Arabella, not Elizabeth, who got the next question right.

'Twelve men walk twelve miles each, how many miles do they walk altogether?'

'One hundred and forty four!' exclaimed Arabella eagerly.

'Very *good* Arabella,' said Miss Ranger. 'My, that was quick.'

Then Patrick, as usual, had to overdo things and show off, spoiling what had been a fun session.

'Perhaps they didn't walk all together but in single file, Miss Ranger. In that case the answer should be none!'

After that they were all made to do sums in their books and had to remain silent for the rest of the lesson.

However, as she pored over her sums, Elizabeth felt well pleased. The hard swotting sessions in her secret hideout were already bearing fruit. Of course, it was

25

annoying to find out that Arabella was ahead of her. Arabella had revised her *twelve* times table! Elizabeth resolved to make that her very next task.

But not today. It was the day of the weekly Meeting and no pupil at Whyteleafe was allowed to miss them. Not that Elizabeth minded. On the whole she very much enjoyed Meetings.

After tea, the whole school trooped into the big hall, which doubled as a gymnasium. There were the twelve school monitors, up on the platform, with the head boy and girl seated at their own special table.

Elizabeth thought how grown up and dignified William and Rita looked, as she took her own place on the first form benches. They had a large book in front of them, known simply as the Book, in which anything important that happened at Meetings was always written down. Elizabeth had read the Book once. It contained many fascinating case histories of pupils who had misbehaved and showed the reasons for it and how their bad behaviour had been cured. She featured in the Book herself, from the days when she had been the Naughtiest Girl in the School!

For the remarkable thing about Whyteleafe School was that the children governed themselves in many respects. The Meeting was like a school parliament, where problems were discussed and solutions found.

ELIZABETH HEARS THE MUSIC AGAIN

But it was also a kind of court, with William and Rita the Judges and the monitors their Jury. Pupils who behaved badly were forced to face up to their wrongdoing in front of the whole school and the Meeting would work out how best the problem could be dealt with and cured. And cured it invariably was, for no child was ever considered worthless, or beyond reform. No one was ever abandoned by Whyteleafe School.

The joint heads, Miss Belle and Miss Best, whom the children nicknamed the Beauty and the Beast, attended the Meetings. So did Mr Johns, the senior master. They were there simply as observers and never took part unless, in very difficult cases, their advice was sought.

Today's Meeting was not an eventful one.

All children who had received money during the week had to give it in. A monitor always brought round the school box. This week it was Joan's turn. As Elizabeth placed some money that her grandmother had sent her into the box, she exchanged smiles with her best friend. She was so proud that Joan, who had not been in the second form very long, was already a monitor.

Elizabeth had herself had a stint as a first form monitor. She had enjoyed being a leader. She looked forward to the day when she might be elected as a monitor again, as William and Rita had once hinted might happen. For the moment, though, she was thinking only of her more modest ambition – to be allowed to go up into the second form!

She would die with shame if she were made to stay down. She would never be able to look Joan in the eye again!

Once the money had been collected up, each pupil in the school was issued with two pounds for the week's spending money. 'Share and share alike' was the school motto.

Then, one by one, special requests for extra money were considered and judged on their merits.

'No, Chloe, we cannot give you extra money for your mother's birthday present. You should have saved up for it, out of your weekly allowance, as all the other children do,' said Rita.

The junior class pupil looked disappointed and sat down cross-legged on the floor again, with the rest of her class.

John, the head of the school garden, was granted some extra money for a trowel, as one had broken. Harriet was given extra stamp money because her large family was in Australia for a year. It was expensive sending all her little brothers and sisters birthday cards and airmail letters.

Colin asked for money for a new tennis racket, as

had been granted to Eileen on a previous occasion.

'That's a difficult one,' said William. 'Rita and I will have to confer with the monitors.'

It took them a while to come to a decision.

William banged a gavel on the table for silence.

'We hope you don't think it unfair, Colin, because we know you have played tennis for the school a few times. But Eileen is a regular member of the team and truly wore her racket out because she practises so hard every day. She has some years to go here and I'm sure will be playing for us much more. You will be leaving Whyteleafe in less than three weeks, as will we. When we go to our upper schools, there will be a different system. For the first time, you'll be allowed to keep any money your parents send you, Colin. If you need a new racket badly by then, we're sure they will help you out!'

'Fair enough,' agreed Colin.

There were no complaints or grumbles this week and the two head pupils began to wind up the Meeting.

Elizabeth's mind was already moving on to other things. Talk of Colin and William and Rita leaving so soon had given her a fresh jolt! It reminded her that there was very little time left before the Leavers' Concert. She longed with all her heart to be a part of that concert, to pay her special tribute to William and Rita from the concert platform. The sweet sad piece she was learning expressed her emotions far better than words.

But swotting for exams every day had not left her all the time she needed for her piano! And Mr Lewis would be expecting to see a big improvement at the next lesson. She had promised him! And, besides, her hopes depended on it.

'It's too late to go to my secret den and do my times tables *today!*' Elizabeth decided. 'I'll do extra piano practice instead. I'll do a whole hour!'

She collected her music case after the Meeting and set off for her usual practice room. But Sophie had got there ahead of her. She was practising the flute. Elizabeth reflected that Sophie would surely be chosen to represent the junior class at the Leavers' Concert. She was a remarkable little player.

'I think I'll be here till bedtime now, Elizabeth,' the younger girl said wryly. 'This is a Grade V piece and I'm only on Grade IV but Mr Lewis says he thinks I can master it.'

'Don't worry, Sophie! I'll go upstairs.'

There was a piano on the top floor, right at the end of a long corridor. It was rather out of the way. Nobody bothered to use that one much.

But when Elizabeth reached the top landing and walked down the corridor, she heard the distant rippling

of the piano being played.

'It's that lovely piece again!' she realized. 'The one I heard yesterday. It must be the same person. Now I can find out who it is.'

The piano was tucked away in an alcove, around a corner at the far end of the corridor. Anxious not to disturb the player, who was in the middle of a delicate diminuendo, she tiptoed the last distance. Then she peeped round the corner . . .

She stared in amazement.

It was Arabella! The fair-haired girl was seated at the piano, playing with the deepest concentration. Her friend, Rosemary, stood alongside her and was turning over the pages for her.

Elizabeth hurriedly drew back. Her heart was pounding. That Arabella should be playing like that!

Her mind could hardly take it in. The conceited Arabella was always showing off. If ever she had something to boast about, she liked the whole world to know.

Why had she never let anyone know she could play the piano so well? Why was she keeping it secret?

Elizabeth stood there, quietly, her body pressed to the wall.

And very soon there came the answer to her question.

CHAPTER FOUR

JOAN STATES HER OPINION

THE MUSIC stopped. Arabella had come to the end of her piece. Then Elizabeth heard Rosemary speak.

'It's perfect now, Arabella. It really is! Shall we go down to our dormy now and I'll test you on your spelling? You know Miss Ranger's said everybody has to pass the English exam before they can go into the second form—'

Out of sight, Elizabeth held her breath in alarm and shrank back harder against the wall. She would creep away, quickly. She didn't want the pair to see her. It would look like spying!

About to turn and tiptoe back down the corridor, she heard Arabella's voice next . . .

'We're not going anywhere, Rosemary. We're staying right here! *You* may think the piece is perfect but I do not. It *is* improving though. Oh, yes, it's definitely getting better all the time!'

She sounded strangely elated. Gleeful.

Elizabeth's attention was riveted.

'But what about the exams?' asked Rosemary, timidly. 'You know I'll die if we can't go up into the second form together.'

'One thing at a time, please. Do stop bleating about the exams, Rosemary,' said Arabella, impatiently. 'Do you really think I've been wearing my fingers to the bone for nothing? Just to throw it all away? Elizabeth's started practising again! I've heard her. Now the play's over I expect she's decided to be in the school concert! Well, she's got such a surprise coming!'

'I bet Mr Lewis can't get over how much practice you've done,' giggled Rosemary. 'All the months you've complained to him about it being boring. He must be amazed.'

'I'm his pet now,' said Arabella, conceitedly. 'Silly old man. He thinks I'm doing all this to please *him*.'

Rosemary knew the real reason.

'It's going to teach Elizabeth a lesson if you're chosen this year instead of her!' She was rather a weak character. She always said what her friend wanted to hear. 'Oh, won't that be fun, Arabella?'

'It's about time she was cut down to size,' said the other girl, fiercely. 'After that, I won't do a stroke of this boring old stuff again, I can tell you. Now, come on, let me play this through again. After that I shall do my scales . . .'

Elizabeth crept away down the corridor. She had heard enough.

All kinds of thoughts and emotions were tumbling through her.

Envy. That Arabella could play the piano so beautifully, when she really tried. She must have a real gift. How could someone so horrid create such a lovely delicate sound?

Realization. Now she knew why Mr Lewis had chuckled to himself about Arabella. He had been chuckling with pleasure. He would have recognized Arabella's gifts as soon as she arrived at Whyteleafe School. For months he had nagged at her to do her piano practice, to no avail. And suddenly she had turned over a new leaf! She seemed to want to please him, after all. How delighted the elderly music master must be at her dramatic improvement. He lived for his pupils and loved to nurture their gifts.

Scorn. How could Arabella be so unkind about Mr Lewis? A silly old man, she had called him. What a horrid thing to say. How mean that she was not really trying to please him! Nor was she working hard for the love of music, or for the honour of playing at the Leavers' Concert. It was all being done simply to spite Elizabeth.

Elizabeth could feel a temper coming on. What a

sneaky person Arabella was. While she had been busy with the school play, Arabella had been swotting away to beat her in class and plotting to steal her piano place as well. Just to get her own back on Elizabeth for being in the play!

It didn't occur to the Naughtiest Girl that Arabella's desire for secrecy was to be expected. She was learning from past mistakes. Encouraged by the feeble Rosemary, she had been cocksure about being chosen for the play. When Elizabeth had been chosen in her place, she had been made to look a fool. She had decided to be much more careful this time.

None of this crossed Elizabeth's mind as, feeling surprised and angry, she walked downstairs, her unopened music case bumping by her side. She didn't feel like doing her piano practice now. She didn't feel like doing anything!

She would go and find Joan. Joan would understand how she was feeling!

She met her best friend coming out of the second form common room with Susan. Gentle Joan could see at once that something was wrong. Making an excuse to Susan, she linked arms with Elizabeth.

'Let's go and sit outside,' she said. 'It's a lovely evening.'

They sat on the school terrace. Elizabeth blurted

out her secret ambition to Joan. Then she told her everything that she had overheard upstairs.

'What a trial Arabella is!' said Joan, sympathetically.

'I don't know what to do now,' confessed Elizabeth. 'The worst thing is that I think she's playing better than I do. I don't know whether I should go on trying.'

Joan frowned and thought about it.

'I don't think it would be very nice if Arabella *were* chosen,' she ventured. 'I wouldn't feel happy knowing that someone was playing at the Leavers' Concert in such a mean spirit. They should want to do it for the honour! And to give the people who are going a happy last memory of Whyteleafe.'

'That's exactly how I feel,' said Elizabeth, eagerly. 'Do you think I should go on trying, then?'

'Of course,' smiled Joan, wanting to make her friend happy again. 'Arabella may be talented but so are you, Elizabeth. She has got a head start at the moment, because you've been so busy since half-term. Given that you're both talented, it's all about who can get the most practice! You must practise and practise, Elizabeth, every spare minute of the day. You must at least give it your best!'

'I will!' promised Elizabeth, her eyes shining. 'I'll practise till my fingers are worn out, Joan. You just see!'

In stating her opinion, Joan knew nothing of the

fright Elizabeth had been given about dropping behind with her school work. She never dreamt that her friend had a secret fear of the coming exams.

As with Julian and all Elizabeth's younger friends, Joan Townsend never imagined that the Naughtiest Girl could have any serious worries about her school work. And Elizabeth was certainly not going to tell her. Her pride wouldn't let her.

'Oh, Elizabeth, I *am* looking forward to your being in the second form,' were her friend's last words to her that evening.

'Yes. It's going to be really good!' replied Elizabeth, stoutly.

That weekend, however, she blanked all thought of school work out of her mind. It was easier that way. She did not once return to her secret hideout in the oak tree.

Her next piano lesson was looming up and the weekend was her last chance of making it a different story from the last one.

She practised non-stop on Saturday and again on Sunday, only taking breaks for meals and other essential activities.

She went back to basics, with Grade I piano scales. Then she worked her way up through the Grades, playing the more difficult scales and finger exercises over and over again. Only then would she tackle her latest piece, the difficult arrangement of *Greensleeves*. She knew that she must achieve technical mastery before she could make it truly expressive.

Julian did not mind at that stage. He was pleased to see that the bold, bad girl had got the bit between her teeth! He was very busy with hobbies himself and also spent a lot of time in the craft room on his wood carvings.

Nor did Kathleen or Jenny or Belinda mind. They were busy, too, revising for the exams, and only felt envious that Elizabeth could afford to be so casual about them.

The only person who minded was Arabella.

She quickly noticed what a huge effort Elizabeth was making.

Arabella had planned to revise for exams this weekend. She was going to try to learn her French verbs and read her English set book. There would be questions about the book in the English exam!

But as soon as she realized what Elizabeth was up to, she abandoned her studies and returned to the piano herself.

'She must have found out! Have you said something to her, Rosemary?' asked Arabella, pouting sulkily. '*Have* you?'

'No, of course I haven't!' said Rosemary, indignantly.

'People must have noticed you coming up here to practise! You can hear it outside when this window's open. Elizabeth must have noticed. You can't expect to keep it secret for ever.'

The new week dawned.

All too soon, in Elizabeth's opinion, it was time for her next piano lesson.

'Hello, Elizabeth!' said Mr Lewis, as she appeared in the doorway, music case in hand. He gave her a warm smile. He had noticed how much practice the first former had been putting in! 'Come and sit down. Let's see how we get on this week, shall we?'

The Naughtiest Girl sat down at the piano. Her fingers trembled slightly as she undid the case and found her music.

This was a lesson in which she must do her very best. She knew she had made great progress since last week but would it be enough? She was longing to ask Mr Lewis about the Leavers' Concert.

'A marked improvement, Elizabeth,' the music master told her, when the lesson was over. 'I can see you have worked very hard this week, to make up for lost time. I'm very pleased with you.'

Elizabeth rose from the piano. As she packed her music away, her throat had suddenly gone dry. This, surely, was the right moment to find out what she wanted to know?

'Please, Mr Lewis—' she began, nervously.

'Yes, Elizabeth?'

'I just wondered if . . . if you'd decided yet . . . about the Leavers' Concert. I mean, who's going to play for the first form? It's not very long now, is it—'

'It certainly isn't!' he chuckled.

He stroked his beard thoughtfully before replying.

Elizabeth held her breath.

CHAPTER FIVE

THE RIVALS

'I CAN quite see that you would like to know, Elizabeth,' the music master said kindly. 'But the fact is, I seem to have a difficult decision on my hands this year. I expect young Arabella has told you that she would like to be picked for the concert, too?'

Of course, Arabella had told her no such thing. Fearing that her expression might give her feelings away, Elizabeth just mumbled and stared at the floor.

She waited to hear what Mr Lewis would say next.

'I want to leave it as long as possible before I make up my mind, Elizabeth,' he went on. 'Apart from anything else, it seems only fair to give you more time to make up lost ground . . .'

Elizabeth's hopes rose. Only to be partly dashed again.

'I must warn you though that I can't make any promises. Arabella has made remarkable progress lately. Quite remarkable. Our lessons together are becoming a real pleasure. One of the great satisfactions of teaching, Elizabeth, is when a pupil at last starts to respond. I must say I am very much looking forward to taking Arabella forward from here . . .' He quickly cleared his throat, suddenly aware that he had been speaking his innermost thoughts out loud. 'As well as you yourself, Elizabeth, of course. And all the other boys and girls I teach.'

In spite of the pain she was suffering herself, Elizabeth's warm heart went out to the music master. Poor Mr Lewis! After this term, Arabella would lose all interest in the piano as suddenly as she had found it! It would be so sad for him.

'So what I am proposing to do is to leave it until the last moment,' he explained. 'I shall have both of you in together, some time towards the end of next week. By then you will both have had your final piano lessons of the term. You will each play your new piece and then we will decide. We can't leave it any later than that!' He chuckled. 'The programmes will need to be run off that weekend, so I will have to make my mind up, won't I?'

Elizabeth nodded eagerly. Her hopes were rising again.

Mr Lewis walked across, opened the door and showed her out. His next pupil was waiting patiently in the corridor.

'I'll see you for your final lesson next week, then. Keep it up, Elizabeth!'

'I shall, Mr Lewis,' she responded firmly.

Elizabeth went on her way, her heart pattering.

All was not lost. Time was on her side. Arabella had been so cocksure, so certain that she was teacher's pet and that she had everything in the bag. But it wasn't like that, at all. Mr Lewis was very fair. He obviously thought that they were evenly matched. He said it was going to be a difficult decision. He was leaving the decision as long as he possibly could – until the week before the concert, in fact. Until just one week before the last day of term!

In the meantime, she had been given another week and a half to improve her playing of *Greensleeves*. In today's lesson, Mr Lewis had helped her to iron out some problems with the tricky part in the middle. There would be one more lesson, next week, to sort out any last-minute difficulties. To add the finishing touches. After that, Arabella had better watch out!

The following day, Arabella had her own weekly lesson. Mr Lewis explained the position to her. After the lesson, she came straight into tea. Elizabeth noticed she looked distinctly bad-tempered. This made her feel cheerful. She remembered the fable of the tortoise and the hare. Well, Arabella had hared ahead of her but now she, the tortoise, had every chance to overtake her.

And that she was determined to do.

44

THE RIVALS

In the days that followed, Arabella's hopes of keeping her ambition a secret were quickly dashed. Some of the first form soon began to notice that both Arabella and Elizabeth vanished away to play the piano in every spare moment. Patrick heard them on the upstairs landing one evening, fighting over the piano. He spread the news around the common room.

'The stupid way girls behave!' he said. 'I knew I shouldn't have come to a school with girls in it.'

Privately he was very put out that he had twice asked Elizabeth to give him a game of tennis. Twice she had made up some feeble excuse.

'If you *must* know,' said Rosemary, unable to hold her tongue any longer, 'it's all because Elizabeth knows that Arabella's going to be picked for the Leavers' Concert this year and she's jealous.'

'You *wish*,' said Julian sarcastically.

Before long, the whole class knew that the two girls were engaged in bitter rivalry for the place on the concert platform. They seemed to have swept all else aside!

It was true that the teachers were no longer giving out prep. But they were leaving it to the children's good sense to revise for the summer exams. These always took place in the last week of term. And neither Arabella nor Elizabeth were ever seen doing private study.

They just seemed to be in the grips of their 'piano craze', as Belinda called it.

'It's all right for Elizabeth,' she said to Jenny one day. 'But Arabella's going to come badly unstuck at this rate. You know how hard she has to work, just to stand still!'

'And she's already the oldest in the form, as it is,' agreed Jenny. 'She should have gone into the second form ages ago. What would happen if she didn't pass her exams? Would they have to keep her down again?'

'Miss Ranger says there's no point in anyone going into the second form if they can't do the work when they get there,' replied Belinda.

'They're both going crazy, if you ask me,' said Jenny. 'Even Elizabeth. I don't think she liked us teasing her about slipping down the form order but it could be a bit more serious if she doesn't watch out!'

In Elizabeth's own mind, of course, it was already serious. Over the next ten days, she woke up each morning fully intending to find time to go to her secret hideout in the oak tree. 'I must do some work for the exams today,' she would tell herself.

But, apart from a session on the Sunday afternoon, she never *did* find time.

The end of summer term was always hectic. There was compulsory strawberry picking to do in the school gardens. There were the knockout tennis tournaments, with all children expected to play in their different age groups. Of course, Elizabeth loved these activities. She loved it when she got to the semi-final of the first form tournament. But it only left time for her vital piano practice and nothing else.

'I'm sorry I haven't been to see you lately,' she told the friendly little robin, on the Sunday. 'You'll see more of me next weekend, when I've got this piano business out of the way. You will see me then, *I* can tell you!'

In her heart, Elizabeth knew that by then it might be much too late. The exams began on the Monday! But she could no longer bear to think about them. Lately, she had begun to console herself with a new thought.

'I can't possibly be made to stay down in the first form, like a baby, if I'm chosen to play at the Leavers' Concert. It's going to be such a grown-up occasion this year, with a real concert pianist coming. Even if I don't do very well in the exams, surely Miss Ranger won't mind?'

So, even on the Sunday, it only needed the distant notes of Arabella's piece starting up to bring Elizabeth scooting down from the oak tree and back indoors to the piano.

By the time both girls had taken their last piano

lessons of term with Mr Lewis, interest in the first form had reached fever pitch.

'How did you get on in your lesson, Elizabeth?' asked Daniel Carter, who had been helping her to practise by turning the pages. Unfortunately Julian had refused. He claimed not to be able to read music. He felt she was now overdoing things.

'Fine,' she replied, confidently. 'I've sorted out that end bit now.'

Martin asked Arabella the same question the next day. He had been taking it in turns with Rosemary to be Arabella's page-turner.

'Mr Lewis seemed very pleased with me,' replied Arabella.

Julian started a sweepstake on the result of the contest, with the children putting in sweets for money.

'Five sweets for four if Arabella Buckley wins,' he announced. 'Three sweets for two if the Naughtiest Girl does.'

Their classmates were all finding it very exciting.

But when the summons from Mr Lewis finally came, the two girls themselves were pale with tension.

It was after tea on the Wednesday.

'Put your music case on the table there, Elizabeth, next to Arabella's,' he said, as she came into the music room. 'I must decide which order you will play in.'

He let both girls run through a few scales, to loosen up. Then he looked at his watch.

'Would you like to play in alphabetical order?' he asked, with a smile. 'You first, Elizabeth.' He meant alphabetically by surname of course. Allan first, then Buckley.

With Mr Lewis turning the pages for her and Arabella seated quietly near the door, Elizabeth solemnly played her piece.

She made no mistakes and put fine expression into it.

'Well done,' nodded Mr Lewis. 'Now you, Arabella, please.'

Looking neat and tidy, as usual, her fair hair brushed and gleaming, Elizabeth's rival took over at the piano. Mr Lewis straightened her music for her.

Now it was the Naughtiest Girl's turn to sit very still and listen.

During the past two weeks, she had heard snatches of Arabella's piece a great many times. She had heard some of the more difficult passages being played over and over again. She knew it was a lovely melody but only now, as she heard it through from beginning to end, did she realize just *how* lovely. It was a pastoral piece, longer and more difficult than Elizabeth's own, and played with deep expression.

49

For a brief time, listening to the music, Elizabeth quite forgot it was Arabella playing and their intense rivalry. She found herself, instead, feeling dreamy, with visions of fields and hedgerows and little wooded hills floating through her mind . . .

Even so, it was still a crushing disappointment when the decision came—

With a brief *Well done* to Arabella, Mr Lewis walked straight over to Elizabeth and placed a gentle hand on her shoulder. In that moment, she knew that she had lost the contest.

'You played beautifully, Elizabeth. But I have made up my mind now. I think we should give Arabella the chance to perform that in public. It distresses me that we cannot have more than one person from each form this year. You deserve to be in the concert after all your hard work. But there it is.'

Arabella was still seated at the piano. She seemed transfixed, radiant. She had surpassed herself. Her own performance had surprised even her.

Elizabeth at once walked across and shook her hand.

'Congratulations,' she said. To hide her disappointment, she gave a wobbly little smile.

For once Arabella did not gloat. She seemed to be in a happy daze.

'Thank you,' she said, politely.

'Thank you, Elizabeth,' echoed Mr Lewis. 'You may leave now if you wish.'

As the music master started to discuss with the other girl the arrangements for the concert, Elizabeth turned her face away and hurried to the door.

She wanted to flee now!

She grabbed the nearer of the two brown leather music cases, not realizing that it was Arabella's. Then she scooped up her music and without even pausing to put it in the case, she shot out into the corridor.

She ran all the way upstairs to dormitory six.

She angrily hurled both the music and the leather case under her bed. Then she flung herself on top of the bed in despair.

Lying there, she could see the pile of school books standing on her white-painted chest of drawers. Standing there accusingly. It was all her revision, still waiting to be done.

She was not going to be in the concert, after all.

And now she was going to fail her exams!

CHAPTER SIX

JULIAN LEARNS THE TRUTH

'CHEER UP, Elizabeth! Have some sweets!' said Julian, as soon as she came down stairs. He produced handfuls of barley sugars and toffees and liquorice allsorts from his bulging trouser pockets. 'Just look what I made on my sweepstake!'

Elizabeth smiled weakly.

Everybody had been very kind.

Joan had been first into the dormitory to comfort her.

'You gave it your very best, Elizabeth. Nobody can do more than that. I'm proud of you. Now all we can do is accept the result.'

Other girls had come into the dormitory and said lots of nice things. Then her friends had dragged her outside and hustled her downstairs.

'Julian's looking for you, Elizabeth!'

'He made lots of sweets out of the sweepstake. Now he wants to share them out with everybody.'

'Come on, Elizabeth, you mustn't brood! Julian wants you to have first pick!'

WELL DONE, THE NAUGHTIEST GIRL!

Elizabeth plucked a favourite stripey allsort from Julian's hand. She popped it in her mouth. Then she chose two black ones and put them in her pocket. Everybody cheered. Then, grabbing sweets themselves, they all hurried off to their evening activities, laughing and chatting happily. The contest between Elizabeth and Arabella was over. It had been very exciting while it lasted!

Elizabeth and Julian were left alone.

From another pocket he produced two extra special expensive-looking chocolates, in crinkly gold foil wrappings. He was determined to cheer Elizabeth up.

'Come on. Have one of these. You've worked too hard. Need to get your strength back, Elizabeth!'

'Who put these in the kitty?' she asked. She unwrapped the chocolate and popped it in her mouth. 'Mmm. Delicious.'

'Arabella! She backed you to win. A sort of insurance policy, I suppose. She's lost them now.'

'Oh, well. That's some consolation,' sighed Elizabeth. She looked at her friend, in mild curiosity. 'However did you end up with so many sweets, Julian? How did you work it all out?'

'Simple,' he shrugged. 'Nobody much likes Arabella but everybody likes you. So I made your odds more tempting than hers and guessed everybody would want to back the bold, bad Elizabeth!'

'But you didn't think I would actually *win*?' realized Elizabeth, her face falling.

She had never seen Julian blush before.

'I had a little listen, a couple of times,' he confessed. 'It was a great surprise but I thought Arabella just had the edge on you.'

'She did,' admitted Elizabeth. 'You were right.'

She looked sad as she spoke. Julian at once tugged her by the hand.

'Come and see what I've got to show you. I've been keeping them a surprise. I want to know what you think. I've been busy, too, you know!'

He led her along to the craft room. Two or three boys and girls were working on their hobbies, completely engrossed. Otherwise, it was empty. Julian led the way to his drawer, in the corner. He took something out, wrapped in tissue paper.

'Look!' he said, lowering his voice. 'Do you like them?'

It was Mother Bear and Father Bear.

They were completed. Julian had sawn the piece of weathered oak in two and stripped off the remaining bark. From the natural shapes of the two pieces he had wrought a pair of carved animals. Father Bear was thick bodied and heavy jowled, with a stern but wise expression. The name WILLIAM was carved at the base. Mother Bear had a gentle face, full of kindness and understanding. Her name had been carved, too: RITA.

The wood had been sanded with great care, then polished until it gleamed. The carvings had taken Julian many hours to complete.

Elizabeth stared at them, in silence.

Julian was so clever. They were beautiful.

But as she looked at those two names, *William* and *Rita*, her own misery resurfaced. It gnawed at her.

William and Rita were leaving next week. Julian had used his time wisely. Now he had a beautiful memento to give them. The beautiful memento that *she* had been planning to give them, her music at the Leavers' Concert, had come to nothing.

She had not used her own time wisely. She had used it stupidly. Now she had nothing to give William and Rita. Instead, she might well fail the exams next week and be kept down in the first form like a baby.

'What's the matter?' asked Julian, glancing at her scowling face. He felt very hurt. 'Don't you like them? Don't you think they're any good?'

'It's not that, Julian!'

'Why are you sulking, then?'

Elizabeth could not bear Julian to think she was

sulking, or jealous in any way.

'The carvings are lovely, Julian. I think you are very clever. It's just that – oh, I've been so stupid—'

Suddenly tears sprang to Elizabeth's eyes and without warning she found herself blurting out her secret fears to Julian.

He looked at her in amazement.

'I am sure Miss Ranger did not mean it about keeping you down!' he exclaimed. 'She was just trying to make you work hard and catch up—'

'But I haven't worked hard and I haven't caught up!' said Elizabeth, in despair. 'And now there's no time left and it's hopeless . . .'

'Of course it's not hopeless, you goose.' He took hold of Elizabeth's arm and led her out of the craft room and into the corridor. He had a feeling that people could hear them, in there! 'Look, if you're really taking this work business seriously, you'd better dash off and do some right now. At least that will make you feel better!' he added, with a grin.

He was humouring her. Privately, he thought her fears were silly.

'I will! I will!' exclaimed Elizabeth. It had been such a relief to tell someone the truth, at last. Julian was so calm about things. She began to feel slightly better. They were quite alone in the corridor now. 'I'll go and do my French verbs. I'm going right now. I've got a secret place, you see. Oh, Julian,' she begged. '*Please* don't tell anyone about this. Promise!'

'I promise. Off you go, then!'

Julian watched as Elizabeth hurried off with a little skip. He shook his head and smiled to himself. The Naughtiest Girl was always full of surprises. You never knew what was going on in her head. That was one of the things he liked about her.

Whistling softly to himself, he went back into the craft room and replaced the wood carvings in his drawer. He was just leaving the room again, when someone spoke.

Daniel had caught snatches of what Elizabeth had been saying earlier. Now, he raised his head from his clay model and spoke to Julian.

'Poor Elizabeth!' Daniel was a sensitive boy. 'She's in a terrible stew about the exams, isn't she? I've never seen her in a state about school work before. It's silly of her not to have done any swotting.'

'Oh, she'll cope all right,' said Julian, airily. 'And don't you go noising this about, either. It's Elizabeth's private business and you're a nosey parker!'

'Sorry, Julian.'

Unfortunately, the very next day Daniel gave Elizabeth's secret clean away.

CHAPTER SEVEN

ELIZABETH HAS A NEW WORRY

DANIEL DID not mean to blurt out Elizabeth's private fears. But next morning, after first lesson, he heard some of the others criticizing her.

'Have you ever seen the Naughtiest Girl so gloomy in class?'

'She looks like the cat that's had the cream taken away!'

'It must be because Arabella won. She's in a sulk!'

'No, she's not!' butted in Daniel, unable to stop himself. 'She's worried about the exams, that's all. She's fearfully worried!'

'What? Elizabeth? We don't believe you!'

'It's true I tell you!' Daniel was determined to defend Elizabeth's good name. 'I heard her telling Julian. She doesn't want anybody to know but she's convinced she's going to fail!'

This titbit of news passed round the class in the course of the morning. They observed Elizabeth's behaviour with interest. She certainly seemed very absorbed in lessons today, taking copious notes all the time. When Julian made a paper dart and sent it skidding across her desk, in the middle of French, she barely noticed. Nor did she raise her head at Mam'zelle's cry.

Zut alors, Julian!

The rumours must be true, then. Elizabeth was really worried.

She was. But her worries were as nothing compared to Arabella's. After her great triumph of the previous day, she had woken up this morning in a state of panic. When Miss Ranger asked her some simple questions on the English set book, the oldest person in the form got every single question wrong. That was the moment when terror struck at her heart.

However, Arabella struggling in class was so commonplace that nobody even noticed. For Elizabeth to be having problems was far more noteworthy.

But by teatime, Elizabeth was in a much more positive frame of mind. Last night, in her secret den, she had revised all her French verbs. She had concentrated hard in lessons today and made lots of notes.

Straight after tea she would return to the oak tree for a good long session with her English set book. She could study it there, in peace. Miss Ranger had said

60

they must be able to quote from it. She would spend at least an hour there and take extra cheese and biscuits with her, she thought, scooping some up and putting them in her pocket.

She hurried up to the dormitory to collect her English book.

She noticed the sheet music flapping about under the bed, where she had hurled it the previous evening. There was to be a Dormitory Inspection tonight.

'I'd better put it away,' she thought, shamefacedly. 'I've no time for piano practice any more.'

As soon as she hauled the music case from under the bed and opened it, she realized that she had picked up Arabella's by mistake! The cases were almost identical but, inside the flap, Arabella had written her name. And there were some chocolate marks, as well.

'When she hid those chocolate peppermints in it!' Elizabeth thought, disapprovingly. 'So she must have *my* case. I'd better go and get it.'

Arabella was still at tea. Her dormitory was empty.

Elizabeth quickly found her own music case. It was standing tucked between Arabella's chest of drawers and her bed. Elizabeth swopped the two cases over. Arabella's current music was lying loose on top of the chest of drawers. Like Elizabeth, she had not bothered to put it away yet.

'So she's not even realized we've got our cases mixed up!' thought Elizabeth. 'Well, as she's never noticed, I won't bother to say anything.'

She hurried back to her own dormitory with her proper case.

'I'll put *Greensleeves* away later. When I tidy up my cubicle for the Dormy Inspection!' Elizabeth decided, dumping the case on her bed. 'I really must rush now. This is wasting time!'

Soon she was ensconced in her tree house once more.

It was all very soothing. The leaves whispered and rustled around her. The big bough was as comfortable as any chair. It had branches protruding on which she could rest her feet, as she lay back against the warm, rough bark of the massive tree trunk.

She knew some of the book quite well and now she must study the remainder. She worked hard for the next hour. She broke off once or twice to feed the robin some biscuit crumbs. She memorized two passages from the book that Miss Ranger had told them were important. She smiled as she saw a squirrel scuttle past.

'Yes, you've got me back!' she told it.

She closed her eyes for a few moments. The doves were cooing again. Oh, she did love this special tree. It was so full of life! Perhaps she would share her secret with Joan one day, and Julian . . .

ELIZABETH HAS A NEW WORRY

Her eyes opened wide. She could hear the murmur of voices, somewhere down below.

She peered down through the leaves. There were two men standing by the country road. They were looking at the tree and talking about it. Then they came and walked round its trunk, immediately beneath her.

They spoke again. This time she could hear exactly what they were saying. She frowned, puzzled by their words.

They were walking away now, in the direction of the village. They glanced back at the tree as they went, still deep in conversation. She could no longer hear what they were saying but she remained deeply puzzled.

'What did they mean about *a big 'un*? And something about some ropes?' she wondered. 'I don't understand . . .'

She remembered the strange white cross that was painted down below. She began to feel a sense of foreboding.

Elizabeth had a new worry now.

Then suddenly, from the direction of the school grounds, she heard her name being called.

It was Julian's voice.

CHAPTER EIGHT

AN EXAM PAPER IS LOST – AND FOUND

'ELIZABETH! YOO hoo! Where are you?' called Julian, hands cupped to mouth.

Harry joined in, as well.

'EE . . . LIZZZZZ . . . ABETH! Come on, wherever you are!'

'Special Meeting!' Julian shouted, to the empty air. 'We've all got to go inside! William and Rita's orders! Special Meeting of the first form!'

Elizabeth peered through the foliage. She could see the boys over by the school field. Now Harry was grabbing Julian's arm.

'Come on, it's no good, Julian,' he was saying. 'William and Rita told us to come straight back if we couldn't find her.'

The Naughtiest Girl watched the two boys run back to the school building. She felt ill at ease.

'Drat!' she thought. 'Whatever are William and Rita having a special Meeting of the first form for?

I don't want to go back inside yet.'

She wanted to stay where she was for a little while longer.

She hated the idea of leaving her tree on its own this evening. Was it something to do with what those men had said? Perhaps. If she stayed for a while, they might come wandering back. They might start talking again. She would listen carefully and try to make sense of what they were saying . . .

But she dare not stay longer. Not when William and Rita had called a special Meeting. Why was it only for the first form? That was very unusual. She had better hurry!

Poor Elizabeth then found herself stuck up the tree in any case – for ten whole minutes! The grounds were very busy at this time of evening. The juniors were coming in from play to have their cocoa. The older pupils were strolling back and forth with cricket bats and tennis rackets. Every time she tried to edge along the bough to climb down the wall and get back into the grounds, she would hear fresh voices!

At last the coast was clear.

She raced over to school, brown curls flying, and made straight for the hall. The doors were open. She slowed down to recover her breath, panting and dishevelled. A figure stepped forward.

'Stop! Elizabeth!'

It was Miss Ranger! She had been standing by the doors, observing the Meeting.

She took hold of Elizabeth's arm and surveyed her.

'There's no point in your going in now, Elizabeth. The Meeting's just ended! Wherever have you been? You know you should wash your face and brush your hair before you come to a Meeting! What *have* you been up to?'

'I – I was just out of doors, Miss Ranger,' she said, lamely.

She peered into the hall. She could hear benches being scraped back and the low buzz of conversation. William and Rita were leaving the platform. There were no monitors with them.

What a short Meeting! Miss Ranger was right. It had just ended.

'Why isn't the whole school here?' she asked, puzzled.

'Because something very unpleasant has happened which concerns only the first form. William and Rita are hoping it can be sorted out quickly. They would rather not have to bring it up at the big weekly Meeting.'

Miss Ranger hurried off then, looking very upset.

'Where did you get to, Elizabeth?' asked her classmates, as they came out of the hall.

One or two of them were looking at her with

considerable curiosity.

'Why didn't you want to come to the Meeting?'

'Are you all right?'

'Of course I'm all right!' replied Elizabeth, impatiently.

She pushed past them and found Julian, who was still in the hall. He was with Kathleen.

'We wondered what had happened to you, Elizabeth,' he said calmly. 'You've missed all the excitement.'

'What excitement? What was the Meeting about?'

'Something terrible's happened,' said Kathleen, her face pale. 'Somebody's stolen one of the first form exam papers.'

Elizabeth was shocked.

'How could somebody do that?'

'It seems they've been printed ready for next week and are in a drawer in the school office,' explained Julian. 'But the Beauty and the Beast counted them this evening and there's one missing. It's a copy of the paper we were all going to get for our English exam. Somebody got hold of their copy in advance!'

'What a cheat!' said Elizabeth, indignantly.

'Well, they haven't got away with it,' shrugged Julian. 'All the questions will have to be changed now. The joint heads must be furious! Shall we do a bit of detective work? That would be interesting.'

'I can't, Julian,' said Kathleen. 'I'm right in the middle of tidying up my cubie for Dormy Inspection. This Meeting's been a real nuisance.'

'Elizabeth?' queried Julian.

Elizabeth was also shaking her head.

Of course, it was terrible that someone had stolen the English paper. And it must be someone in their class! Who could it be? Normally, she would have been fascinated to do some detective work with Julian. They often solved things together.

But this evening she had something else on her mind. Something that was worrying her very much. A matter that she felt was of supreme importance.

She had quite a different mystery to investigate.

'I'm sorry,' she said. 'I want to go and talk to somebody about something. In fact, I'm off there right now.'

Kathleen looked puzzled as the Naughtiest Girl rushed away.

'Don't forget, Elizabeth! We've got Dormy Inspection, tonight. Don't go and disappear again!' she called out.

Julian just smiled and scratched his head. Dear Elizabeth. What was she up to *now*? It seemed to be something new. At least she didn't seem to have exams on the brain any more!

AN EXAM PAPER IS LOST – AND FOUND

Elizabeth left the school building and hurried to the stables. She wanted to speak to the stableman. He was a real countryman and a fount of knowledge.

She would ask him what a white cross on the trunk of a tree might mean. She would also ask him if he had ever put ropes round a tree and if so, why. We'll rope her up first thing in the morning . . . That's what the men had said.

Of course, she mustn't let him suspect that she was asking about any *particular* tree. He might wonder how she knew so much about the oak tree when it didn't belong to Whyteleafe and was not even in the school grounds. She shouldn't really know anything about it at all!

But she had to speak to him, urgently. It was *her* tree and she had to know if anything were going to happen to it in the morning.

She desperately hoped not. Perhaps the stableman could give a simple explanation. Then she would hurry back and tidy up her cubicle for Dormitory Inspection.

Silly old Dormitory Inspection! This was much more important.

'Where has Elizabeth got to *now*?' said Miss Ranger, angrily. 'Her behaviour is very strange at the moment.'

The Dormitory Inspection was in full swing.

Once a fortnight, the dormitories at Whyteleafe School were checked for tidiness. The class teacher concerned would accompany Matron on a tour of inspection.

All the other girls in number six stood to attention by their cubicles. Beds had been beautifully made, rugs straightened. The number of items on top of chests of drawers was limited to six, as school rules ordained. So far, Matron and Miss Ranger had been well pleased.

But now they were staring into Elizabeth's empty cubicle in annoyance. It was a mess. And the Naughtiest Girl herself was nowhere to be seen! Where was she?

She was climbing the stairs at that very moment, taking them slowly, one at a time. She was deep in thought and feeling trembly.

The stableman had not been at the stables. It had taken her some time to track him down.

But now, at last, she had the answer to her questions.

'It's not fair! It's horrible!' she raged to herself, over and over again. 'It's not in the least bit fair and I shall make them stop!'

She was already forming a plan in her mind.

She walked into dormitory six, her face very tense and pale.

In something of a daze, she noticed that Miss Ranger

and Matron were standing in her cubicle.

'Elizabeth! This is a disgrace!' said Matron. 'Look at all the books on your chest of drawers—'

'And don't add your English book to the pile!' scolded Miss Ranger, as she saw Elizabeth take the small volume out of her pocket. 'Your school books should be in your desk, not up here!'

'I've been reading it this evening for the exams,' protested Elizabeth.

She was still feeling in a daze.

'You should have been tidying up your cubicle!' said Miss Ranger, standing by the bed. 'What's your music case doing, just dumped on top of the bed? And you haven't even bothered to put your music away.'

The teacher gathered up the score and opened the brown leather case, intending to slip it neatly inside. But there was something in the way.

'Even your music case needs a tidy-up,' she complained.

She pulled out a crumpled sheet of paper that had been stuffed just inside the case.

She straightened it out and stared at it in disbelief.

'Elizabeth!'

The teacher's shocked cry brought everybody running to the scene.

Miss Ranger was holding something aloft, between

thumb and forefinger. She was waving it in front of the Naughtiest Girl.

Gasps of surprise echoed round dormitory number six.

It was the stolen exam paper.

'What was this English examination paper doing hidden in your music case, Elizabeth?' asked Miss Ranger.

The Naughtiest Girl gazed at the printed sheet in total astonishment. It was an exam paper, sure enough. Even from here she could see a list of questions about the English set book. She was dumbstruck.

'Is that why you have been reading so avidly this evening?' continued the teacher, in acid tones, glancing at the book in Elizabeth's hand. 'To plan your answers to the exam questions in advance?'

'No!' protested Elizabeth, angrily. 'Of course not, Miss Ranger!'

'I repeat. How did this exam paper come to be hidden in your music case?' asked the teacher.

Matron was trying to usher the other girls out of earshot. But they were hanging on to every word.

'Answer me, Elizabeth!' rapped Miss Ranger.

'I have no idea!' exclaimed Elizabeth, hotly.

'Come, come, Elizabeth. Think carefully before you speak. You must have *some* idea of how a stolen exam paper could be found in your music case,' said the teacher calmly. 'Just think about it for a moment. It must have got there somehow, must it not?'

Elizabeth's sense of outrage began to subside. Miss Ranger's comment was perfectly fair. How *had* it got in her case? She took a deep breath, to try to calm herself. It had been such a shock! The little girl frowned deeply for a few moments as she tried to think clearly.

Slowly, the truth dawned on her.

'Well, Elizabeth?'

The Naughtiest Girl had become pink with excitement.

'I – I think I know the answer,' she said. 'You see, my music case has been in somebody else's possession all day.'

'Somebody else's possession?'

Elizabeth's room-mates glanced at each other, uncomfortably. What a silly thing to say! The music case had been lying under her bed all day. They had noticed it there and wondered if she had forgotten about Dormy Inspection tonight.

'Whose possession, Elizabeth?'

'I – I'd rather not say, Miss Ranger.'

It sounded very feeble.

The teacher glanced at her watch.

'It is nearly bedtime. You are to tidy up your cubicle,

74

this instant. Then if, as you say, there is somebody else involved in this matter, you are to bring them to the staff room before you go to bed. I will wait to see you there. If for any reason you cannot find this other person, there is nothing more we can do about it tonight. Miss Belle and Miss Best will see you in the morning.'

It was clear, realized Elizabeth, that Miss Ranger found it very difficult to believe her story.

'Yes, Miss Ranger!' she replied, confidently.

Very soon the teacher would see that her story was true.

CHAPTER NINE

ELIZABETH DISAPPEARS

ARABELLA SAT primly on her bed in pyjamas, pretending to read a book. The curtains of her cubicle were drawn. She knew that would hardly deter Elizabeth. She was expecting her at any moment.

Next door, in room number six, Matron had supervised Elizabeth while she tidied up her cubicle. In those ten minutes, the dramatic news had spread like wildfire. The boys alone, away to their own quarters by then, knew nothing of the unfolding drama. But the news had very quickly reached Arabella's dormitory.

The excited chatter had raged all round her.

'The paper was in Elizabeth's music case! She was caught red-handed!'

'She tried to pretend someone else used her music case today. Miss Ranger says she'd better produce them!'

'I knew it was funny the way she didn't come to the Meeting! I *said* that was weird.'

'Poor Elizabeth! We knew she was in a bad way!'

'It was silly of her to waste all that time on the piano!'

'It's not a *bit* like Elizabeth to cheat. I'm so amazed!'

Arabella, already in pyjamas, had quickly drawn the curtain round her cubicle. She had peered inside her music case in horror.

The truth had dawned. They must have got their cases muddled up yesterday. Elizabeth had come and swopped them back this evening without checking inside and now everybody thought that she had stolen the exam paper.

Suddenly, now, the curtains parted.

'So there you are!' exclaimed Elizabeth, stepping into the cubicle. 'Just the person I want to speak to.'

Arabella's heart was thumping. She noted the fierce glitter in Elizabeth's eye.

'Am I?' she asked innocently, looking up from her book. 'And why would that be, Elizabeth?'

'You know perfectly well! It's about you stealing that exam paper and then putting it into *my* music case by mistake!' hissed Elizabeth. 'We've got to go and see Miss Ranger straight away. The two of us. You had my music case all day, not your own! You will have to confess to her.'

'I'm sure I don't know what you're talking about!' exclaimed Arabella, deliberately raising her voice. 'How dare you accuse me of stealing something. I haven't touched your silly music case!'

It brought Rosemary on to the scene at once.

'Elizabeth's saying I haven't had my music case all day, Rosemary. She says I've been using hers! Did you ever hear such nonsense?'

'Arabella's case has been here since yesterday evening. I've seen it!' protested Rosemary. 'Look, there it is! It's never budged.' She pointed to its position on the floor tucked between bed and chest of drawers. 'Whatever would she want *yours* for?'

Elizabeth stared at Arabella in disbelief. Arabella was refusing to own up. She must by now be perfectly well aware of what had happened. But she was not going to admit it.

'So you don't agree that you sneaked into the school office some time today and took that exam paper?' asked Elizabeth, scornfully. 'And then crept up here and hid it in the music case by your bed? Thinking it was your own! If I hadn't come in here after tea and swopped it for your proper case, the exam paper would still be there *now!*'

Arabella had gone very white.

Rosemary, thinking it was because of the outrageous things being said, turned on Elizabeth.

'You came and swopped it, did you?' she jeered. 'Did anybody see you?'

'Well, no. It's just that I . . .'

Elizabeth's voice trailed away. For the first time she

realized that she had not one single witness to support her story.

'It's just that you are sick with jealousy at Arabella being chosen for the concert!' said Rosemary, finishing Elizabeth's sentence in her own way. 'And not content with stealing the exam paper, you're now trying to pin the blame on *her* so that you'll play in the concert instead of her!'

Arabella was breathing heavily. She was racked with emotion.

Elizabeth had guessed the truth exactly. And, faced with the fierce candour of what Elizabeth had been saying, Arabella had come within an ace of confessing. Until Rosemary's words had reminded her of how much she stood to lose . . .

The Leavers' Concert! Her great moment of triumph was just one week away. So many times, Elizabeth had had the last laugh and she, Arabella, had been made to look stupid. All that would change now. People would look up to her. They would respect her. Perhaps they would even start to like her, the way they always liked Elizabeth. She had surprised herself, how well she could play the piano! She had worked so hard for her moment of glory next week. Nothing was going to rob her of that!

'I really don't know anything about a silly exam

paper, Elizabeth,' she said, her face expressionless.
'You seem to have made a mistake.'

The Naughtiest Girl looked at her, sorrowfully.

'You're a hopeless case, Arabella,' she said quietly.
'There is no point in talking to you.'

She left and returned to her own dormitory.

The room fell silent at her arrival but she cared not.

She went into her cubicle and drew the curtains.
Then she lay down on top of the bed, still fully clothed.

She lay on her back, head resting on hands, staring at
the ceiling. Outside, dusk began to fall. None of
her room-mates came to see her, or said goodnight. Her
friends were too embarrassed. Poor Elizabeth, they
were thinking. So worried about the exams, to creep
into the school office like that. And caught red-handed!
Trying to pretend that it must have been somebody else!

Miss Ranger, too. Waiting in vain for Elizabeth to
appear with 'somebody else'. Thinking exactly the same
thing.

'They will have to think what they like,' decided
Elizabeth, with a deep sigh. 'I can't prove my story is
true and I expect Arabella will never confess. Never
ever! But then life is not fair. No. Nothing is fair!'

The amazing sequence of events since teatime had
convinced her of that. She was not thinking of her own
plight but something of even greater concern.

ELIZABETH DISAPPEARS

Soon she heard steady breathing from every corner of the dormitory. The others were all asleep at last. It was time to put her plan into action.

When the rising bell sounded next morning, Elizabeth did not appear from her cubicle.

Kathleen walked over and pulled back the curtain.

'Wake up, Elizabeth. It's late!'

Then she gasped.

The sun's morning rays slanted across Elizabeth's neat, empty bed. Kathleen could see at once that it had not been slept in.

Elizabeth had disappeared.

CHAPTER TEN

A HUE AND CRY

'ELIZABETH'S RUN away!' cried Kathleen, in great alarm. 'Look, she must have done. Her bed's not been slept in!'

The others rushed over.

'I don't believe it!' exclaimed Jenny, in astonishment. 'Perhaps she just got up early!'

'No, Kathleen's right.' Belinda checked the bed carefully. 'Look, the covers have never been pulled back. And do you notice something? One of the pillows has gone.'

'Yes – and so's the spare blanket!' realized Jenny.

They all looked at one another in horror. Poor Elizabeth! Overcome with shame, she had run away from Whyteleafe School. They had a sudden vision of her, wandering the dark country lanes with blanket roll and pillow, sleeping in ditches, trying to make her way back home.

'We should have been nicer to her,' moaned Kathleen. 'We should have been more understanding . . .'

As the word spread to the next dormitory, other

pyjama-clad girls thronged in. They gathered round Elizabeth's empty bed, pale and shocked. Nobody looked more shaken than Arabella who already had dark rings under her eyes from a bad night's sleep.

The first form girls held an emergency meeting on the spot.

'She'll never get home safely! It's more than a hundred miles. And she hasn't any money!' said Tessa.

'I wonder where she slept last night?'

'Some smelly old barn, I expect.'

'What should we do?' asked Belinda. 'Do you think we should go and report this to the Beauty and the Beast straight away?'

'It's not like Elizabeth to run away when she's got a problem!' decided Jenny, after giving it due thought. 'Perhaps this is just one of her pranks, to give us all a fright! Perhaps she's hiding around the school somewhere.'

'And if we go and tell the joint heads, she'll be in even deeper trouble,' realized Kathleen. 'More than she was already!'

'Yes, you're right!' exclaimed Arabella, eagerly. 'We mustn't worry any of the teachers about this at the moment. That would be silly. Let's search the school buildings.'

'Perhaps she's asleep in one of the storerooms?' suggested Rosemary.

WELL DONE, THE NAUGHTIEST GIRL!

The first form girls rushed to get dressed. Then they fanned out in all directions, scouring the school buildings.

Arabella scurried up and down the corridors, looking in the empty classrooms, opening and shutting each door with growing unease. Nobody had managed to find Elizabeth yet. Where *was* she?

'I expect she'll turn up at breakfast-time,' said Rosemary, to comfort her friend. 'She hasn't any money and she's bound to be starving hungry. It's not your fault, Arabella, if Elizabeth Allen has decided to do something idiotic.'

These were not the words to bring comfort to Arabella.

Elizabeth did *not* turn up at breakfast.

Sitting in the dining-hall, staring at that empty place, Arabella's serious unease turned to panic.

The Naughtiest Girl really had run away! And it was all her fault. She should have confessed about the exam paper while she still had the chance. Now Elizabeth felt hopeless about things and was sure that nobody would ever believe her. If only Rosemary had not butted in, thought Arabella, she might have admitted the truth. She had been on the point of doing so.

Now she was seized by a feeling of dread. Elizabeth

could be in danger. Something dreadful might have happened. Supposing she had been run over? And really, when she thought about it, Elizabeth was not *that* bad. She had her good points, after all. As she toyed with her breakfast cereal, Arabella's eyes kept straying to the door. How lovely it would be to see the Naughtiest Girl come strolling in through that open door, right now, laughing at them all and enjoying her silly joke . . .

Come back, Elizabeth, she kept thinking. *Oh, do please come back!*

But still Elizabeth did not appear and by the end of breakfast there was a great hue and cry. Daniel went racing off to see if she might be sleeping in the school stables.

'We must go and see the joint heads right away,' said Joan, turning pale, as soon as Kathleen had explained things to her. The second form monitor had looked across and noticed that her best friend's place at table was empty. 'Oh, poor Elizabeth! I am perfectly certain she would never have stolen an exam paper. She must be feeling very angry and upset at being misjudged.'

'Hear! Hear!' agreed Julian.

Kathleen reluctantly rose to her feet. She was beginning to feel very guilty.

'Will the heads ring the police, do you think, Joan?'

'I'm sure they will,' replied Joan. She looked across at

Julian. 'Do you want to come with us, Julian?'

He just sat there, spooning down the last of his cereal. He shook his head. He was frowning.

'I might follow on in a minute,' he muttered. 'I'm just trying to have a good think.'

There was a great buzz of excitement round the dining-hall as Joan and Kathleen went off together. By now, nearly everybody knew what had happened. Elizabeth Allen's bed had not been slept in. It looked as though she must have run away from school! Now Joan and Kathleen were going to report it to Miss Belle and Miss Best. The joint heads would have to telephone the police!

Julian put his spoon down, his brow deeply furrowed.

The Naughtiest Girl was always full of surprises. Even so, he found this one most baffling. If she *had* taken that exam paper she would have owned up at once except that she would never have taken it in the first place! She had been unjustly accused. But in that case, the last thing she would do would be to run away. Not the bad bold Elizabeth. She would stay to fight her corner, to the bitter end. It was such a riddle. There must be some other reason for her vanishing trick. Something different altogether . . .

He was trying hard to remember a remark she had made two days ago. It was to do with her swotting for

86

the exams, without wanting people to know how worried she was.

'Got it!' he whispered suddenly. 'I remember what she said.'

I've got a secret place, you see!

A secret place! Was that why they couldn't find her for the Meeting yesterday? And was this now the explanation? Had the crazy Elizabeth been up all night, swotting for the exams in some secret hideout?

'And still there!' thought Julian. 'Probably fast asleep! But where is it?'

At that moment, Daniel returned.

'She's not in the stables,' he said, miserably. 'I think it was very catty of those girls last night, not accepting her word. Elizabeth would never cheat. No wonder she was upset. But it's all my fault,' he confessed. 'You see, I spilt the beans, Julian. About her being so worried about the exams. That's why they didn't believe her. I didn't mean to but I did.'

'Oh, do shut up, Daniel,' said Julian, absently. 'Can't you see I'm trying to think?'

When Joan and Kathleen arrived at the school office, they were amazed to see that Arabella had beaten them to it.

'Come in, please,' called the joint heads.

They each sat behind a desk and Miss Ranger stood by the window. She had arrived earlier to report back on the matter of the stolen exam paper. The culprit had been found.

'Elizabeth Allen? Oh dear. How very disappointing!' the joint heads had exclaimed.

Arabella, accompanied by Rosemary, was already in there. They were both seated.

Joan and Kathleen stared at them. Why had Arabella got there ahead of them? She seemed to be crying. Rosemary looked distressed, too, and was biting her lip.

'Please ring the police, Miss Belle!' Arabella was pleading, tearfully. 'I'm so worried about Elizabeth! I'm so frightened that something could have happened to her. And if it has, it's all my fault. I drove her to this. I drove her into running away! I could have owned up about the exam paper when I had the chance and I didn't.'

'You have owned up now, Arabella,' said Miss Belle, calmly. She nodded towards some more chairs. 'Sit over there, please, Joan and Kathleen. You may join us.'

The two headmistresses were very composed.

'We will have to contact the authorities, which will be very bad for Whyteleafe,' Miss Best began. 'Before we do so, we need to be quite sure the child has run away. Have you all had a good look for her?'

'We've searched high and low, Miss Best,' replied Kathleen, only just beginning to take it all in.

Elizabeth had been telling the truth all along. Somehow her music case *had* been in somebody else's possession yesterday. Arabella's! And it was Arabella who had stolen the English exam paper. She had come and confessed to Miss Ranger and the joint heads!

As Miss Belle and Miss Best asked further probing questions, Kathleen found it difficult to take her eyes off the fair-haired Arabella. It was strange to see her vain, doll-like face streaked with tears, to see her genuinely caring about somebody else for the first time, somebody other than herself.

'*Please* telephone the police,' she implored again.

The joint heads glanced at one another. It seemed that they had no choice.

'We'll speak to them right away,' said Miss Best, reaching out for the telephone.

'No!' cried a boy's voice, from the doorway. 'Please don't ring them yet!'

Julian walked eagerly into the room. Everybody stared at him.

'I might be able to find Elizabeth! I've got a hunch but I'll need some time! Could you just give me fifteen minutes, please? We can ring the police after that!'

Miss Best took her hand away from the telephone.

She glanced at Miss Belle and then nodded. They both knew that Elizabeth's friend was a brilliant boy.

'Very well, Julian. Fifteen minutes.'

'And not a minute longer,' added Miss Belle.

CHAPTER ELEVEN

WELL DONE,
THE NAUGHTIEST GIRL!

'DON'T WORRY, big brown moth. Don't worry, friendly little robin!' whispered Elizabeth, as down below the men took the ropes off the back of the lorry. *Don't worry, chattering squirrels and cooing doves and busy little insects and creepy-crawlies!* 'This is your house. I won't let them chop it down, I promise!'

Hidden in the oak tree, Elizabeth had the fierce light of battle in her eye. She had slept fitfully in its warm boughs. It had been a much lighter sleep than usual. The sleep of a soldier at the battlefront, ready for the enemy and poised for action. And since dawn she had been wide awake. She knew that the woodmen might start work very early. That was why she had not dared to sleep in her proper bed last night.

They had arrived at long last, not as early as she feared but early enough. They parked their lorry on the wide grass verge below and began to sort through their equipment. She was ready for them. She tensed every muscle now. She was preparing to make her stand.

At the same time, Julian was walking briskly round the grounds of Whyteleafe School. He was looking urgently about him. It was a chance remark of Daniel's that had given him his clue.

The stableman hasn't seen Elizabeth since last night, Julian. She was asking him all about trees or something.

So that was the person Elizabeth had rushed off to speak to last night. The stableman. To ask him about trees. Why *trees*?

Trees . . . secret place.

Could Elizabeth's secret hideout be in a tree? And in that case, which one? What sort of tree?

And then, in a flash of inspiration, Julian had remembered the piece of oak that Elizabeth had found him. That splendid piece of oak for his wood carvings . . .

But where had it come from? She had never explained. He had occasionally looked for oak himself and never found any. The reason being, as far as he could recall, that there were no oak trees in the school grounds. But there must be one somewhere, one that he had missed . . . And could that be where she had made her secret hideout?

He walked round to the back of the stable block, looking up at all the trees there. Then he stared at the meadow beyond. There was not an oak tree in sight. He hurried back by way of the cricket pitch. He was almost giving up hope.

Then, suddenly, he saw it.

'It's been right under my nose!' he realized. 'Only it's growing *outside* the school, on the other side of the wall. That's why I didn't notice it!'

He stood back and surveyed it. Elizabeth could have got into that tree by climbing up the boundary wall . . .

'And she has!' gasped Julian as Elizabeth's head suddenly poked out of the middle of the tree. She was shouting! She seemed to be looking down at some people in the road.

'Go away, please! Go away and take your horrid chainsaw with you! I'm staying here and I'm not going to budge. I won't let you cut this tree down. Never, ever! Don't you realize lots of little creatures live here? This is their home!'

Julian goggled for a moment – and then came to a swift decision. He turned away and sprinted back towards the school buildings. At top speed. His fifteen minutes was almost up.

'Julian!' exclaimed Miss Ranger, in relief, as he burst back into the school office, his face shining. 'You have some news?'

'I've found her!' he exclaimed. 'I know why she

disappeared now. It had nothing to do with the exam paper or anything like that!'

He told them all that was happening.

At first there were cries of joy and relief that Elizabeth had been found safe and well. But, after that, some anxious frowns appeared on the teachers' faces.

'That beautiful old oak tree? The one that we can see from the school grounds? It's being taken *down*?' said Miss Belle. 'Oh, Miss Best, we must do something about it. And quickly.'

'We certainly must,' agreed Miss Best. 'I will ring the tree department as soon as the council offices open.'

She rose to her feet and rapped out an order.

'Julian, you are to return to the tree immediately. You are to join Elizabeth there. She needs reinforcements. Under no circumstances are either of you to come down from that tree until we give you permission. And please tell Elizabeth that refreshments are on their way.'

'Oh, Julian, I'm so glad you turned up when you did,' said Elizabeth. 'I was getting so tired of arguing with those men. I don't think I could have stuck it out much longer up here. Not on my own. Not without any breakfast.'

'Another hour should do it,' grinned Julian.

Seated comfortably in the tree, the two friends munched the last of the delicious sandwiches that Joan and Arabella had brought out to them. They offered the robin a few crumbs.

It was morning break and quite a crowd of boys and girls was starting to gather below.

The woodmen had long since retreated. They had parked their lorry some distance away down the road. They were sitting in the cab, drinking tea from a flask, waiting helplessly for further instructions.

'They tried to tell me the tree needed to come down for a road widening scheme!' said Elizabeth, indignantly. 'A beautiful healthy tree like this with no disease at all! Who wants the silly road widened? Drivers can go a bit slower as they always have done and still have a lovely old tree to look at.'

The tree department people agreed with Elizabeth entirely. It turned out that the powers that be hadn't got all the correct paperwork, so the men weren't allowed to cut the tree down. Within the next hour, an official arrived and pinned a notice to the old oak. It was an emergency Tree Preservation Order. It would go to appeal, of course, but now Miss Belle and Miss Best were involved, Elizabeth was confident the tree would survive.

The doves cooed and all the little birds sang, as

though in gratitude. Elizabeth's heart sang loudest of all as, aching with tiredness, they were given permission to descend from the tree at long last. Everybody cheered.

'Well done, Elizabeth!'

Well done, the Naughtiest Girl!

CHAPTER TWELVE

GOODBYE TO WILLIAM AND RITA

NEVERTHELESS, ELIZABETH had been in breach of school rules. The big oak tree was out of bounds. She had visited it not once but several times. And she had spent an entire night away from her dormitory, causing everyone great alarm and anxiety. That was a most serious offence.

At the big school Meeting the next day, it all had to be written down in the Book. It was the last Meeting of the summer term and the last one ever for William and Rita. There were serious matters to discuss and the head boy and girl were determined that they should be dealt with fairly and wisely. All their conclusions would be written in the Book, offering help and guidance to future Meetings after they had gone.

'As soon as you suspected the tree was in danger, Elizabeth, you should have reported it to a monitor,' said William. 'Even though, to do so, would have meant confessing that you had been out of bounds.

Another time, you must try not to take matters into your own hands.'

'Yes, William,' agreed Elizabeth, contritely. 'I'm sorry.'

'On the other hand,' said Rita, busily writing in the Book, 'this was one of those very rare occasions when breaking a school rule had a beneficial outcome. If you had not been exploring the tree in the first place, you would never have discovered that it was to be felled. It would have been lost. Although you should not have acted alone, your action was brave and so that must go in the Book, too.'

The Meeting had to deal with Arabella's crimes, too. That was more difficult.

At the behest of the joint heads, Miss Ranger had started giving Arabella some extra lessons in preparation for Monday's English exam. She would have to spend the entire weekend on difficult exercises. There would be a completely new paper set, of course. The Beauty and the Beast had reasoned, correctly, that the girl must be beside herself with panic to have stooped so low. She clearly needed help. At the same time, cheating was a serious offence at Whyteleafe School and so was letting someone else take the blame. These were things that the Meeting must deal with.

There was also the very difficult matter of next week's

Leavers' Concert to think about. Should Arabella still be allowed to play – or should Elizabeth take her place?

'Why did you practise so hard for the concert, Arabella,' asked Rita, as the fair-haired girl stood up, 'when you should have been working for your summer exams?'

'At first I just wanted to be chosen to spite Elizabeth,' replied Arabella truthfully. 'She always seems to be better at things than me and then she laughs at me. I don't know why nobody likes me and everybody likes Elizabeth.'

'Elizabeth can be very naughty but she has a warm heart and that is why people like her,' explained Rita. 'She cares for others whereas you are sometimes thought not to.'

'It wasn't a bit warm-hearted of her to make such a contest of it,' complained Arabella. 'She knew I was better than her but she started practising so hard, I didn't dare slack off after that. I was so worried about the exams but I *couldn't* let Elizabeth beat me and I knew she wanted to. It was my big chance to shine, you see,' she blurted out. 'I did so want to be chosen. That – that was the only reason I took so long to confess about the exam paper.'

'Is this true, Elizabeth?' asked William. The whole school was listening, in fascination. 'That you knew

Arabella was better than you but decided to make a battle of it? Even when you both had exams coming up?'

For the first time, Elizabeth felt a twinge of shame.

'Yes, it is true,' she said, hanging her head. 'I did realize Arabella was better, quite early on. But I still wanted to beat her. Even though I'd been in the school play and she hadn't. And even though it meant skimping all my revision. And so, in a way, I suppose I stopped her revising, as well.'

Sitting down again, next to Julian on the first form benches, Elizabeth began to think deeply about things.

Poor Arabella! Elizabeth had been working hard and was starting to lose her fear of the exams. But she could tell that Arabella was as worried as ever. It must be dreadful to be the oldest in the form and always struggling near the bottom.

On the platform, with the other monitors, Joan put her hand up.

'Please, William, don't just blame Elizabeth! I think it was wrong of me but I heartily encouraged her at the time.'

'And I encouraged Arabella!' exclaimed Rosemary, jumping to her feet. 'I tried to mention the exams sometimes but most of the time, I just egged her on.'

The head boy looked from Joan to Rosemary and nodded.

'Thank you both for speaking up,' he said. 'There's an important lesson to be learnt here. The rest of the school, please take note. We always want to please our friends, don't we? We like to say to them the things that they want to hear. But sometimes the thing that is *best* for them is the very last thing that they want to hear. The finest friendship you can give someone is to stand up to them sometimes and tell them when you think they are doing the wrong thing.'

Joan at once nodded agreement. Rosemary sat down, feeling very ashamed at the way she always pretended to agree with Arabella, even when she knew she was wrong. Elizabeth glanced at Julian admiringly. He had told her several times that she was overdoing things with the piano business.

Rita wrote all this down. Then she, in turn, addressed the school.

'There is something else I would like to point out. To both Elizabeth and Arabella. But it applies to the rest of us, too. It is very easy to care about people whom we like. To care equally for those people whom we don't like is much more difficult but is something we must strive for.'

Shyly, Kathleen put her hand up.

'Please, Rita, Arabella was really upset when she thought something had happened to Elizabeth. Even though she doesn't like her! She was crying.'

The Naughtiest Girl's eyes opened wide at this surprising piece of news. She turned to look at Arabella but the other girl turned her head away, embarrassed.

'Thank you for pointing that out, Kathleen,' said Rita. 'And this brings us to the final business of the Meeting. We have given everything a good airing and now we have to decide about the Leavers' Concert. Should Arabella still be allowed to represent the first form or should Elizabeth take her place?'

'This is going to be a very difficult decision,' added William. 'Rita and I will talk it over with the monitors.'

Everybody on the platform went into a huddle. There seemed to be a long argument going on. Elizabeth sat very tense and still. So did Arabella. All around them the hall buzzed with conversation, as the boys and girls discussed amongst themselves which of the two girls should be allowed to play.

Then William banged the gavel on the table for silence.

'We are finding it impossible to reach agreement,' he announced. He gazed towards the back of the hall where, as always, Miss Belle, Miss Best and Mr Johns sat in on the Meeting. They never joined in unless their advice was sought. 'We would like the heads to tell us what they think.'

Miss Belle at once rose to her feet. She was smiling.

'While you have been discussing this difficult problem, we have been discussing it, too. We have decided that you should let Elizabeth and Arabella use their own good sense in the matter. Let them discuss it together privately. Let *them* decide which of them should play at the Leavers' Concert.'

It was the end of summer term at Whyteleafe, the very last day of the school year. William and Rita and the others were leaving today! Exams were over and the results posted on the board.

Elizabeth had passed! She would be going up into the second form next term! She would be reunited with Joan. She would be going up with Julian and Patrick and Kathleen and Belinda and Jenny . . . and Arabella! Somehow Arabella had managed to scrape through the English exam and had passed in maths, and French as well. She had failed some other papers but because of her tremendous progress in music this term had been given some useful bonus marks for that instead. So she was being allowed into the second form.

'As a matter of fact, I really like my piano practice now,' she had confided to the music master. 'I never

104

realized how satisfactory it could be, to find out that there's something one is really good at!'

Mr Lewis was delighted.

It was time for the Leavers' Concert.

He was up on the platform in the hall now, smiling at Sophie as she waited nervously with her flute. She would be the first to perform. All the parents had arrived and the hall was crammed full.

The girl from the junior class soon got over her nerves. She gave a faultless performance. Everybody applauded. William and Rita, sitting in the front row, sat very still. They glanced at each other, moist-eyed, for they knew that this concert would be their last memory of Whyteleafe.

'And now,' announced Mr Lewis, 'to represent the first form we have one of our most gifted pupils. Arabella Buckley.'

Sitting between her parents, near the front, Elizabeth watched Arabella as she walked on to the platform. She put her music in place on the grand piano which had been brought into the hall for this special occasion. How magnificent it looked. Arabella looked quite small against it. She looked different today, thought Elizabeth, her fair hair brushed and gleaming, a spot of colour in each cheek, her eyes sparkling.

As she started to play a deep hush descended over

the audience. The pictures came again to Elizabeth, conjured up by the music. Those lovely visions of green fields, grass blowing, clouds scudding across blue sky, wooded hills . . . What a fine player Arabella was!

William and Rita listened, enraptured.

All too soon it was over.

Children from other classes came and went. Richard played his fine new piece. Then Courtney Wood, the well-known concert pianist, performed for the rest of the programme, as planned.

It had been a wonderful Leavers' Concert this year and yet, for Elizabeth, it was Arabella's music that lingered in the mind. Had the head boy and girl enjoyed it as much as she had? She did hope so!

Afterwards, she and Julian went to say goodbye to them. They were deeply touched when Julian presented them with the little wood carvings.

'They are quite beautiful, Julian!' exclaimed Rita.

'Father Bear rather looks like me, doesn't he?' laughed William in delight.

He turned to face Elizabeth and smiled approvingly.

'So you and Arabella sorted it out then? How did you decide?'

'It was easy,' replied Elizabeth. 'I just thought Arabella's piece would be the best memento for you, better than mine actually. I – I'm just sorry that I haven't got anything of my own to give you.'

'But we heard your music drifting out one evening, Elizabeth, and that was lovely, too,' said Rita quietly. 'I will never be able to hear *Greensleeves* in future without its reminding me of you.'

Elizabeth blushed with pleasure.

'Naughtiest Girl in the school – Best Girl in the school!' laughed William. 'You have no need to give us a memento—'

He bent and kissed her on the cheek. Then Rita did likewise.

'Memento? Please don't be silly!'

'Dear Elizabeth! How could we ever forget you?'

BONUS BLYTON

Enid Blyton has been one of the world's best-loved storytellers for over 70 years. Her interest in writing began as a child, and before she loved receiving letters from the children who read her books, she enjoyed working with them as a teacher. The Naughtiest Girl stories are inspired by real schools and experiences. Turn the page to learn more about Enid as a child and as a teacher. Afterwards, you might like to write about your school and teachers and the people in *your* class!

THE LIFE AND TIMES OF
ENID BLYTON

11 August 1897	Enid Blyton was born in East Dulwich, London. Two brothers are born after her – Hanly (b. 1899) and Carey (b. 1902)
1911	Enid enters a children's poetry competition and is praised for her writing. She's on the path to becoming a bestselling author . . .
1916	Enid begins to train as a teacher in Ipswich. By the time she is 21, she is a fully-qualified Froebel teacher, and starts work at a school in Kent.
1917	Enid's first 'grown-up' publication – three poems in *Nash's Magazine*.
June 1922	Enid's first book is published. It's called *Child Whispers*.
1926	Enid begins editing – and writes – the phenomenal *Sunny Stories for Little Folks* magazine. (She continues in this role for 26 years!)

1927	So vast is Enid's output that she has to learn to type. (But she still writes to children by hand.)
1931	Having married Hugh Pollock in 1924, the couple's first child, Gillian, is born. Imogen, their second daughter, was born in 1935.
1942	The Famous Five is launched with *Five on a Treasure Island*.
1949	The first appearance of *The Secret Seven* and of *Noddy* mark this year as special.
1953	Enid moves away from *Sunny Stories* to launch *Enid Blyton's Magazine*. She is now renowned throughout the world – she even established her own company, called Darrell Waters Limited (the surname of her second husband).
1962	Enid Blyton becomes one of the first and most important children's authors to be published in paperback. Now, she reaches even more readers than ever before.
28 November 1968	Enid dies in her sleep, in a nursing home in Hampstead.

Enid's death wasn't the end of her remarkable legacy. In the 1970s, the Famous Five became TV stars (Noddy having already hit our screens in 1955). In 1996, the Enid Blyton Society was formed so that fans across the world could share their enthusiasm for Enid's work (www.enidblytonsociety.co.uk) In 2012, the Famous Five celebrated 70 years of continuous publishing, with special editions featuring covers by top illustrators, led by Quentin Blake. New book, film and merchandising deals are being struck all the time. Enid's work is definitely here to stay!

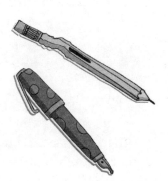

MY SCHOOL DAYS:
AN INTERVIEW WITH ENID BLYTON

What did you like most about school?

I loved school, every minute of it. I loved learning. The things I liked at kindergarten were the things I have liked best all my life – stories – music – nature – and games.

What do you remember about school?

I remember everything about it – the room, the garden, the pictures on the wall, the little chairs, the dog there, and the lovely smells that used to creep out from the kitchen into our classroom. I remember how we used to take biscuits for our mid-morning break and swap them with one another – and how we used to dislike one small boy who was clever at swapping a small biscuit for a big one.

What was your best subject?

Essay and composition and story-writing.

What about your worst?

Sums. I hadn't the right kind of brain for figures and I used to look on in awe when I saw other boys and girls doing the most complicated sums.

We know you loved stories. Tell us about some of your favourites?

My favourite book as a child was called *The Princess and the Goblin* by George Macdonald, and also loved *Coral Island* by R. M. Ballantyne. Other books I enjoyed include:

Alice in Wonderland and *Alice Through the Looking-Glass* by Lewis Carroll.

Black Beauty by Anna Sewell (even though parts of it were sad).

The Water Babies by Charles Kingsley.

Arthur Mee's Children's Encyclopedia – which I read from end to end. Nature books. Annuals. Magazines, too.

Myths and legends from all around the world.

I liked poetry – even when I didn't really understand it.

I quite liked comics – but found they were like sweets – you sucked them for a few minutes, then they were gone, and you didn't think about them any more.

Were there any books you *didn't* enjoy?

I didn't like *all* stories. Some I found dull and boring, just as you do. There were no real children as characters, and it was children I badly wanted to read about. There were no lively conversations in the books. Nothing to really make me laugh.

The responses to those questions are based on comments by Enid Blyton in her autobiography, *The Story of My Life*, © Hodder & Stoughton, 1952.

WHAT THEY DID AT
MISS BROWN'S SCHOOL

In 1920, Enid Blyton became a governess to the four Thompson children, whose ages ranged from four to ten. The family lived in Surbiton, in Surrey, in a house called 'Southernhay'. Enid had a small room which overlooked the garden, and it was there that she wrote many of her stories. Enid's tiny class often had lessons outdoors in the summer months.

Enid was very popular with her students, because her lessons were both practical and creative. She worked with them to put on performances for which they made props, costumes and invitations – and even sold tickets.

In 1941, she published a long story called 'What They Did at Miss Brown's School', which was divided into monthly episodes. It's been hard to find for many years, but you can read extracts in these new editions of the Naughtiest Girl books. The character of Miss Brown and her tiny class is very much based on Enid Blyton and her school at the Thompsons' . . .

Here's the eighth extract . . .

WHAT THEY DID AT
MISS BROWN'S SCHOOL

September. Planning for the Spring-time.
Bulbs for the Classroom.

WHEN THE children came back to school at the beginning of September, they were delighted to see that Miss Brown had set out a good many of their sea-shells on cards.

'You must print the names neatly underneath and let me see how many you remember,' said Miss Brown. 'And Mary shall hang the seaweed up outside the window and tell us each day what the weather is going to be!'

John saw that Miss Brown had put up a big blank Nature Chart on the wall. It was headed WINTER TERM.

'Oh, Miss Brown!' he said, making a face, 'winter term! How horrid that sounds! Here we are still in summery weather, with the blue sky above and the sun so hot that I can't wear a coat – and you are going to make us keep a chart for the WINTER TERM!'

Miss Brown laughed. 'You will find it is winter when the middle of November comes,' she said, 'and our swallows and martins are gone, and there are few flowers left and few leaves on the trees!'

'I like the spring best of all,' said Mary. 'I wish we could have a bit of spring in the middle of winter, Miss Brown – wouldn't it be lovely?'

'Well, I don't see why we shouldn't,' said Miss Brown unexpectedly. 'How would you like to smell the delicious sweetness of hyacinths in December, and to see the gold of daffodils and the red of tulips in the New Year?'

'Oh yes, let's!' cried the children.

'How can we do that?' asked Mary.

'We'll plant all kinds of bulbs in bowls,' said Miss Brown. 'If we do them this month the first of them will be out by Christmas, and we shall really feel that spring can't be very far off, even if snow is thick on the ground!'

'I can bring two bowls, Miss Brown,' said Susan. 'I've got two of my own at home.'

'Well, if you will all try to bring the bowls I will buy the bulbs and the fibre to plant them in,' said Miss Brown. 'A friend has kindly given me some money to spend on flowers – and I think it would be a fine way to spend it – to buy bulbs that will give us flowers in the middle of winter.'

Well, that week the children brought six bowls, big

and small. There were two blue bowls, two green ones, a yellow one and a brown one. Miss Brown was so pleased. She brought out from the cupboard four tall glass vases, nipped in at the neck, which she said were hyacinth glasses.

'They are rather like acorn glasses but much bigger,' said Susan. 'Do we just put the bulb at the top, here, Miss Brown?'

'Yes, and we put water in up to the neck,' said Miss Brown, 'with a bit of charcoal to keep the water sweet – and the hyacinth bulb will put its roots out into the water and grow well.'

'Can we come with you to buy the bulbs?' asked John. 'What are you going to buy?'

'Well, we will have some white Roman hyacinths for one bowl,' said Miss Brown. 'They will be out in December. We will also have a bowl of paper-white narcissi – they flower very early too.'

'And let's have some red tulips!' begged Mary.

'Very well,' said Miss Brown, 'and we must have some ordinary hyacinths as well – we'll get bright blue for this blue bowl.'

'And can we have some daffodils?' asked Peter. 'I do love those.'

'Yes – this deep, tall bowl will do for those,' said Miss Brown. 'They grow a bit leggy.'

'That leaves one empty bowl,' said Susan. 'Can I choose something for it, Miss Brown? I'd like crocuses!'

'Yes, crocuses would be lovely in that little green bowl,' said Miss Brown. 'And we will grow red, white, blue and pink hyacinths in the glasses – one for each of you! We can set those on the window-sill and watch them. We shall not need to put them away in the dark, as we shall with the other bowls.

'Let's go and buy the bulbs tomorrow!' cried John. So the next day they set out to get them. They soon arrived at the same shop where they had bought their garden seeds and the shopman was pleased to see them.

'I've some fine bulbs,' he said, 'all ready prepared for growing early. It's no good growing ordinary garden bulbs in bowls, you know, Miss Brown – they won't come out any earlier than the ones out of doors. You want to buy specially prepared bowl-bulbs.'

'Yes, I know,' said Miss Brown. 'Now, children, here are the hyacinths – big, round, fat bulbs with purplish-brown scales. Feel them and choose one good solid one for yourselves, any colour you like. Be sure the bulbs don't feel soft or pulpy – they will not grow if they do.

Susan chose a fat hyacinth bulb that would have a blue flower. Mary chose a pink one, Peter chose a white one and John had a red one. The shopman put each into a small bag and wrote the colour on in pencil.

Miss Brown had chosen fifteen small Roman hyacinth bulbs. They were not nearly so big as the children's bulbs. 'But, you see,' said Miss Brown, 'Roman hyacinths are almost like white bluebells – not really like the big hyacinths you see in gardens. The flowers are smaller, so the bulbs are smaller.'

Then she chose six fine blue hyacinths. That was for another bowl. Then she and the children picked out six brown-skinned daffodil bulbs, and six neat red-brown tulips.

'There are the paper-white narcissi,' said the shopman, bringing some bulbs that looked rather like small daffodil bulbs. 'These will flower very early. How many will you have?'

They chose six. And then they looked at the little rounded crocus corms.

'These are not bulbs but corms,' explained Miss Brown. 'A corm is quite solid inside, but if you cut a bulb open you would see that it is more like an onion, and right in the middle you would fine the hidden leaves and flowers, waiting to grow. Now, we'll have twelve of these crocus corms – purple crocus, please – as the yellow corms do not seem to be very good.

Then they bought a bag of brown fibre to grow the bulbs in, and off they went back to school, very happy indeed.

The next day they set to work to plant all their bulbs. They did have a fine time. Miss Brown emptied the fibre into a big enamel bowl.

'Now,' she said, 'you must pour water into the fibre, and work it about with your hands until it is thoroughly wet. It is just wet enough if you can squeeze it in your hands without water coming out. When it is all ready, pack it neatly into the bowls, about half-way up.'

This kept the children very busy. How they loved to feel the wet fibre in their hands! At last they had wetted it enough, and they put some in the bowls.

'And now we will plant the bulbs,' said Miss Brown. 'Mary, put the Roman hyacinths into that green bowl. Settle them firmly on the fibre. Then neatly pack the bowl full to about an inch from the top. John, do the same with the narcissus bulbs. Peter, plant the daffodils, and Susan, you can do the tulips.'

Very soon four bowls were packed full. Miss Brown planted the blue hyacinths, and then the children found that there was not enough fibre for the sixth bowl!

'It doesn't matter,' said Mis Brown. 'We can grow crocuses in stones and water very nicely indeed – and we can put them straightaway on the window-sill, and watch them grow instead of putting them away in the dark! John, go outside and collect about thirty little pebbles and wash them.'

John soon came in with thirty clean pebbles and he arranged some of them at the bottom of the crocus bowl. Miss Brown poured water in. It just reached to the top of the pebbles but no more. Then John set the twelve crocus corms neatly on the stones. After that he packed the rest of the stones around the corms, so that only the tiniest bit of the little white shoots at the top could be seen.

'Good!' said Miss Brown. 'Now we will do our other hyacinth bulbs – the ones we want to grow in the hyacinth glasses.'

Mary filled each hyacinth glass with water. Then the children each put a bit of charcoal in the water and carefully set their fat bulbs at the top of the glass. They rested there nicely, just touching the water underneath.

'Set them on the window-sill,' said Miss Brown. The crocuses can go there too. I will put the other bowls away into a dark, airy cupboard. There is one in the kitchen. Carry the bowls, children, please.'

There was a little dark cupboard off the kitchen that had plenty of fresh air from an outside ventilator. Miss Brown set all the bowls on a shelf there.

'They must stay for some weeks in the dark,' she said, 'so that they will make plenty of root-growth. Then, when their roots are well-grown, and the shoot is beginning to sprout, we will put them in the classroom.

Once a week we must feel the fibre, and if it is dry, we must give a little water.'

It wasn't long before the hyacinths in the glasses put out tiny white roots into the water. After that they grew very quickly, and soon the whole water was full of roots! Susan's had the first and biggest roots. She was very proud.

The crocus corms grew roots too. Miss Brown took up a few of the top stones and showed the children how the roots were twining around and between the pebbles. She added a little more water, for the warmth of the classroom was drying it up.

'The white crocus shoots look like white animal's teeth growing up,' said Susan. And so they did!

'It was very exciting when Miss Brown brought the bowls of bulbs out into the classroom in November. They had all grown fine strong roots and were now sending up fat green shoots.

'Miss Brown!' said Susan, one day in December, 'look! Is this a bud in the paper-white narcissi – down here in between the leaves?'

It was! Everyone was very pleased, and when they saw how quickly the leaves and buds grew they were astonished. Then the Roman hyacinths put up buds too, and as Christmas drew near the children anxiously watched to see if the flowers would open.

All their own hyacinths were budding too, but would not be out till the New Year. The tulips would be out just at the beginning of January and the daffodils later still.

The week before the holidays the white Roman hyacinths were out in full flower! How lovely they were – just like white bluebells, with a very sweet scent indeed. They made the whole classroom smell nice. Then the paper-white narcissi opened their sweet-smelling stars, and the classroom smelt twice as sweet! Really, it was lovely!

'You were right when you said that we would have a bit of spring in the middle of winter, Miss Brown,' said Mary, sniffing the hyacinths. 'This was a lovely thing to do! And how pleased I shall be when the purple crocuses are all out too, and the tulips shine red, and the big hyacinths hang out their scented bells! And how lovely the classroom will look when the bowl of golden daffodils is out!'

'The only thing I'm sorry about is that we can't use our bulbs again for bowls next year,' said Peter. 'The man said they wouldn't be any use.'

'Ah, but we can plant them out in the garden and they will flower for us there! said Miss Brown. 'We will have a little bulb-corner, shall we – and plant our bowl-bulbs there each year! Isn't that a good idea!'

More classic stories from the world of

Enid Blyton

The Naughtiest Girl Wants to Win

Elizabeth is furious when new girl Kerry Dane is made head girl over her friend, Emma. Kerry is a nasty piece of work, but how can The Naughtiest Girl prove it?

A sparkling new edition of this classic story, with an introduction by Cressida Cowell (author of the *How To Train Your Dragon* books), behind the scenes facts and stories, and new illustrations by Kate Hindley.

And remember, there are ten books in the series to enjoy!

More classic stories from the world of

Enid Blyton

The Famous Five

The adventures of Julian, Dick, Anne, George and Timmy have been delighting readers for over 70 years. There are twenty-one adventures – full of mystery, suspense, danger and surprise.

More classic stories from the world of

Enid Blyton

The Famous Five Colour Short Stories

Enid Blyton also wrote eight short stories about the Famous Five. Here they are, in their original texts, with brand-new illustrations. They're a perfect introduction to the gang, and an exciting new way to enjoy classic Blyton stories.

More classic stories from the world of

Enid Blyton

The Secret Seven

Join Peter, Janet, Jack, Barbara, Pam, Colin, George
and Scamper as they solve puzzles and mysteries,
foil baddies, and rescue people from danger – all without
help from the grown-ups. Enid Blyton wrote fifteen
stories about the Secret Seven. These editions contain
brilliant illustrations by Tony Ross, plus extra
fun facts and stories to read and share.